I0584274

THE SNUGGLY
SATANICON

EDITED, INTRODUCED AND TRANSLATED

BY

BRIAN STABLEFORD

THIS IS A SNUGGLY BOOK

ISBN: 978-1-64525-081-4

CONTENTS

THE SNUGGLY
SATANICON

Brian Stableford's scholarly work includes *New Atlantis: A Narrative History of Scientific Romance* (Wildside Press, 2016), *The Plurality of Imaginary Worlds: The Evolution of French roman scientifique* (Black Coat Press, 2017) and *Tales of Enchantment and Disenchantment: A History of Faerie* (Black Coat Press, 2019). He has translated more than three hundred volumes from the French, mostly in the genres of *roman scientifique*, *contes de fées* and Romantic and Symbolist fiction.

His recent fiction includes the visionary science fiction novel *The Revelations of Time and Space* (2020) and its sequel *After the Revelation* (2021); the last in his long series of "Tales of the Genetic Revolution," *The Elusive Shadows* (2020); and the comedy fantasy *Meat on the Bone* (2021), all published by Snuggly Books.

INTRODUCTION

THIS volume completes an eccentric triptych of sorts, following on from *The Snuggly Satyricon* and *The Snuggly Sirenicon*. It is more selective than its predecessors, having a much wider range of titles to choose from, of greater average length, and its attention is not as concentrated on the *fin-de-siècle*, nineteenth-century literary fascination with the symbolic figure of Satan having been a central feature of the French Romantic Movement. A thriving tradition of "literary Satanism" was pioneered in the 1820s that continued throughout the century and into the twentieth, which subjected the figure to closer and more skeptical scrutiny than the theologians of the past, attempting a more clinical analysis of the idea.

Nineteenth-century writers had no difficulty finding abundant imaginative fuel for calculated revision and perversion of, and wry dissent from, the scarecrow image of Satan cultivated by the Church as an active agent of moral terrorism, no longer licensed to kill by means of imaginary testimony in witch-trials, but still dangerous. In an interesting minority of cases, a few of those philosophical revisionists found grounds for some sympathy for the Devil, frankly opposing the Church's construction of a personification of evil.

The English Romantics had laid the foundations of potential sympathy for Satan, notably in William Blake's remark that John Milton had been "of the Devil's party without knowing it" in his remarkable characterization of Satan in *Paradise Lost*. That allegation was taken up by Percy Shelley, who regarded the Miltonic Satan as a heroic rebel against unjust divine tyranny—a problematic kind of hero who came to be called "Byronic" by analogy with the most successful and widely read of all the English Romantics, in France as well as in England. Byron incorporated suggestions of Satanism into the lifestyle fantasy he popularized, which became the foundation of French Dandyism as soon as the English had sent its key exemplars into permanent exile and elected to follow a much blander etiquette. Although Byron's friend George Brummell was often credited with modeling the dandy's style of dress, having remained in England while Byron fled to Italy, and then moving to France when disgraced in his turn, it was Byron who provided the ideology behind it, and it was Byronic "Satanism" that Charles Baudelaire had in mind when he declared, sternly, that henceforth, his "only colors would be black."

English Romanticism contrasted somewhat in that regard with German Romanticism, which had a different imaginative tradition to draw on, in which a ley position was held by Johann Spies' *Faustbuch* (1587), one of the most influential literary works ever penned, which reconfigured the notion of Satanic pacts in its depiction of the intercourse between the scholar Faust and the diabolical Mephistopheles. Reinterpreted in Elizabethan England by Christopher Marlowe, it achieved its most significant modern reconfiguration in J. W. Goethe's two-part dramatic work (1808 and 1832), adapted in several operatic versions. The widespread influence of that ambivalent archetype focused uneasy sympathy not on Satan himself but on humans motivated to commit themselves to his care and custody, although one line credited to Mephistopheles—usually translated as "Why, this is Hell, nor am I out of it," achieved iconic status as a reconstitution of the possible relationship between the world and the Devil's Imperium.

The French Romantics had earlier precursors of their own to draw upon, most notably Jacques Cazotte's pioneering novella *Le diable amoureux* (1772; tr. as *The Devil in Love*), in which a demon becomes infatuated with a young man and assumes the form of a seductive young woman in order to be near him and assist him, but that influence was probably outweighed by German exemplars—E. T. A. Hoffmann was also enormously popular with the French Romantics—and confused with a more general Byronism. In truth, Satan had far less influence on Lord Byron than Lord Byron had on the image of Satan, whose personification as a loathsome Dantean monster, although still available and tempting as a literary instrument, found an increasingly common counterpart in a suave and urbane dandy, able to engage in casually witty dialogue with his multitudinous Fausts.

The most significant work of early French Romantic literary Satanism was Alfred de Vigny's long poem "Éloa, ou La Soeur des anges" (1824; tr. as "Eloa"), in which a female angel who falls madly in love with an extraordinarily handsome male angel chooses to accompany him to Hell, even though she was not involved in his rebellion. That work had a powerful influence on many later writers, adding to Cazotte's influence in assisting the peculiar eroticization of a significant fraction of French Satanic fantasies. It also helped to reconfigure the role typically played by angels as adversaries of the Adversary, complicating their battle for hegemony over human souls. It was soon supplemented by Alphonse de Lamartine's *Le chute d'un ange* (1838), clearly inspired by it, which argues that angels are far more likely to be led to damnation by amour than by pride, and added a further important modification to their depiction in French Romantic fiction.

The influence of "Eloa" is also very evident in the work of S. Henry Berthoud, who produced a short novel, *Asrael et Nephta, Histoire de Province* (1832), in which a male angel who has fought against the rebels is tricked into believing that his beloved has been cast into Hell with Satan and only realizes his error too late, becoming the most reluctant of demons before returning to earth on a mission of perverse self-salvation. Berthoud, in imitation of Jakob Grimm, had earlier attempted to collect local folktales in his native Flanders, many of which featured the Devil as an everpresent threat to human existence, and when the tales he had collected proved unsatisfactory he became a prolific manufacturer of "fakelore" pastiches, in which he often nudged the traditional Devil in the direction of more Romantic imagery. Three of them are included here as samples of a curious microsubgenre.

The first prose masterpiece of French Satanic fantasy, Gustave Flaubert's *La Tentation de Saint Antoine* (tr. as

The Temptation of Saint Anthony), begun in the 1840s, had a long period of gestation, and it was only at the third attempt that the author finally thought it sufficiently representative of his genius to warrant publication in 1874. The train of thought that led to its strangely ambivalent account of Satan's struggle to doom Saint Anthony built upon several more orthodox precursors discovered among the author's juvenilia, written in the late 1830s and belatedly added to his canon, one of which is included herein as a sample of the burgeoning obsession.

Very few of the works in the burgeoning Romantic tradition ever became entirely sympathetic to Satan, although those that did gradually became more flamboyant as the century progressed, the tentative black alleluia of Charles Baudelaire's combative poem "Les Litanies de Satan" (1857; tr. as "The Litanies of Satan") eventually being supplemented by Anatole France's spectacularly sentimental anticlerical novella "L'Humaine Tragédie" (1895; tr. as "The Human Tragedy"), in which a virtuous monk discovers, to his great dismay, that the only friend he has in the corrupt world is Satan. France went on to pen the microsubgenre's second great prose masterpiece, the novel *La Révolte des anges* (1914; tr. as *The Revolt of the Angels*). Whether they were sympathetic or not, however, what marked all Romantic fantasies dealing with Satan was their attempt to carry forward Milton's mature psychoanalysis of Satan, a sensitive appreciation of the motive wellsprings of opposition to God and the tactics of the temptation employed to lure humans away from God's alleged notion of virtue.

Inevitably, most of the representations of Satan contained in the present volume, as in the whole of nineteenth-century French literature, accept Satan for what he was forced to be by cruel definition: an embodiment of evil. Many of them are even content to take it as read that Satan must, therefore, be a thoroughly nasty piece of work, but even the stories meekly accepting that judgment tend to have a certain Miltonian and Byronic unease about them. However sanctimonious they are, they are frequently compelled to a certain admiration for Satan's perseverance and ingenuity—and also, with increasing frequency, his sense of humor: a capacity for irony and sarcasm that has an artistry of its own. Even in stories in which Satan remains a foul monster reeking of brimstone, authors working in the Romantic era had no alternative but to try to understand him a little better, to give him a little credit where credit was due, no matter how fervently they exploited their own resources of authorial ingenuity to thwart and re-damn him in the end. The conflict going on in many of these stories is not so much a matter of good versus evil as the striving of a nagging literary conscience against the temptations and sins of narrative convention.

It is, of course, fated that Satan always loses in the battle for the throne of Heaven, although even that assumption was brazenly channeled in the remarkable prelude to Catulle Mendès' masterpiece *Gog* (1896), which suggests that Jehovah was actually defeated and dethroned, but that the successful Father of Lies has pretended otherwise for reasons of long-term strategy. In the stories assembled in this particular Satanicon, only

Pyrrhic victories of successful temptation and individual human damnation are possible for him, although having won the first of those small victories by putting one over on poor Eve, the hereditary taint of original sin makes things much easier for him thereafter, and in the ongoing contest between his age-old cunning and mere human ingenuity, the odds always seem tilted in his favor.

In the Romantic world-view, however, even in its most sexist variants, there is always a residue of sympathy for the daughters of Eve and at least a slight suspicion that His judgment in her case and theirs was unduly harsh—and, indeed, that an eternity of torture in Hell for relatively minor infractions of Ten Commandments, at least half of which are clearly not fit for purpose, is incompatible with modern theories of penology. When Romantic writers elect to take up the pen against Satan's pitchfork, therefore, it is not necessarily him that they are really attacking, but the law that he represents, for which he is not responsible. Often, of course, that does not prevent him from relishing his role and playing his absurd part to the full, with malicious gusto, but that kind of competitive spirit, although not necessarily admirable, is at least understandable, and not immune to whims and mutations of conscience.

It is important to remember that Romanticism was in decline throughout the nineteenth century, corroded by the positivism that had similarly begun as a rebel movement and rapidly faced a Satanic condemnation of its own, but which embarked upon a long guerilla war for hegemony over the human mind that made steady and inexorable progress, while Romanticism only maintained the upper hand in the battle for hearts. Byronic dandyism was already on the defensive when Baudelaire adopted it, and he probably would not have wanted it any other way, being an archetypal "oppositional personality" who would always far rather be wrong than orthodox.

Although it was Théophile Gautier rather than Baudelaire who defined literary Decadence, using him as its cardinal example after first, with duly paradoxical conscientiousness, arguing that the label was inappropriate, it was the latter who was thus appointed the great champion of a species of Romanticism that reveled in its own erosion by the tide of history, as it crumbled into the morass of vulgarity. That awareness of decadence confers a kind of ironic elegiac quality to some of the stories herein written by Baudelaire's contemporaries—Flaubert, Jules Janin and Léon Gozlan, for instance—which became increasingly obvious in the work of the next generation of writers to whom the torch was passed in the *fin-de-siècle*. Inevitably, that shift in the literary current was reflected in the dealings that writers had with Satan. While Satan always retained his multitudinous versatility, his roles were corroded by an increasing flippancy as it became increasingly difficult to take him seriously, either in scarecrow guise or in his affectations of dandyism. The Satans we meet in stories by authors such as Catulle Mendès, Jules Richepin and Félicien Champsaur, therefore, while still maintaining a recognizable kinship with the Satans of Charles Nodier and S. Henry Berthoud, have aged noticeably, perhaps wearing their decadence proudly, with Byronic and Baudelairean pugnacity, but stigmatized by it nevertheless.

Not all Satanic fantasies feature an individual Lucifer, of course, many focusing on lesser devils, and there are even a few that recall the fact that the word "satan" was originally a trivial noun rather than a proper one. The ultimate derivative of "Eloa" featured in the present collection is Lucie Delarue-Mardrus' "A Woman in Hell," which offers a significant antidote to Byronic posturing, carefully spiced with a cynical satire beyond that of Catulle Mendès and Félicien Champsaur, and thus possessed of an admirable distinctiveness.

Although the previous volumes in the triptych to which this collection belongs did not exhaust the literary resources of the satyr and the siren in nineteenth and early twentieth-century France, it would not be easy to assemble another Satyricon or Sirenicon with the same exemplary value as those thematic showcases. A Satanicon, however, can only be a small section cut out of a vast pattern; it would not be hard to put together a similar collection of equal substance without any overlap, and at least a third, or even a fourth. By the same token, the context into which a collection of Satanic short fiction fits, surrounding it with much longer works and an abundance of poetry, is far richer. The present Satanicon, in consequence, can hardly avoid a suspicion of arbitrarinesss. It cannot cover the entire range of attitudes and narrative strategies in the way that the *Snuggly Satyricon* and the *Snuggly Sirenicon* aspired to do.

Even so, the present volume is hopefully a worthy companion to its predecessors, and also a useful supplement, providing an additional piece of a much vaster jigsaw comprised by the chief imaginary motifs of modern literature, helping to provide a broader glimpse, and hence a more accurate appreciation, of a bigger picture. And even though it will not be easy to think of another viable theme beginning with S, there is surely a moral obligation of all thinking people to resist the tyranny of alliteration, just as there is to rest the tyranny of divine injustice, so the sequence need not stop here, if temptation summons, and the fruit seems luscious. It would, in any case, be grotesquely inappropriate to sign off the introduction to a Satanicon with an *adieu*.

—Brian Stableford

THE SNUGGLY
SATANICON

DEAD MAN'S DALE

by Charles Nodier

IT would have taken a lot in 1561 for the road from Bergerac to Perigueux to be as good as it is today. The great forest of chestnut-trees which still surrounds it was even more extensive, and the roads were even narrower. At the place where it seems to be suspended over a deep gorge, which was then called Hermit's Dale, the mountain slope that bottomed out in that valley was so steep and perilous that brave men scarcely dared to tackle it even in broad daylight. At eight o'clock on the eve of the first of November of that year—All Saints Day—it would have been completely impractical to attempt the feat, because the premature rigor of winter had added further dangers to the natural difficulties.

The sky, obscured from daybreak till sunset by a harsh wind-driven drizzle, mingled with snowflakes and hailstones, allowed nothing to be distinguished but the gloomiest horizons. Just as the darkness of the Heavens was confounded with the shadows of the Earth, so the sounds of the air were also mingled with those of the earth, in a horrible manner which made travelers' hair stand on end. The storm-wind, increasing from moment to moment, moaned like the voice of a crying child or a mortally-wounded old man crying out for help. It was impossible to tell whether the most frightful of these lamentations came from the height of the clouds or the echoes of the precipice, for the plaints of the forest, the neighing of stabled horses, the shrill whirr of dry leaves whipped up by whirlwinds, and the clatter of dead branches broken by the tempest all ran together. It was terrifying to hear.

The black and hollow vale of which I spoke just now opposed to that, at one point, a striking contrast, a fixed brightness, large and flamboyant, which expanded from below like the plume of a volcano; and from the open door with two battens that gave access to it, gusts of laughter emerged capable of cheering up despair. That is because it was the forge of Toussaint Oudard, the black-smith, who had attained the age of forty without making a single enemy. He was joyfully celebrating the feast-day after which he had been named by the light of his furnaces and in the midst of his workmen, intoxicated by pleasure and wine.

It was not that Toussaint had never violated the sanctity of a saint's day to shoe a horse or put an iron hoop on a wheel, at least when he had to deal with an unexpected emergency suffered by travelers from abroad, and then he accepted no payment for his labor. Even so, his forge never relented in its ardor during the most scrupulously-observed holidays, because it served as a beacon—especially during bad weather—for unfortunate passers-by gone astray, who always found a welcome there. Whenever the peasants of the dale were called upon to describe the house of Toussaint Oudard, son of Tiphaine, the phrase most commonly applied to it was "Charity's Inn."

Toussaint suddenly came into the large kitchen adjoining the forge, where a few pieces of meat supplied by huntsmen and the butcher were roasting over a fire so fervent that the forge might have envied it, within the ample spread of one of those fine old fireplaces that seems ideally designed to serve the purposes of hospitality.

"See how well it's going," he said, cheerfully, addressing himself to an old woman sitting on a stool beside the hearth, her soft and serious features shining in the bright light of a copper lamp with three burners, which was secured by a bracket to the ancient plaster, stained black by smoke and by time. "It's my opinion that all the little ones are in bed and that a jolly flock of young women from the dale will provide you with good company for the night ahead, as usual. God preserve me from allowing it to be troubled by the cries of my children, long-deafened by the noise of the anvil, who wouldn't hear one another unless they howled like wolves. I've just sent them to my bedroom, where their cries won't reach you. Will you be so kind, mother, as to send us one of your maidservants with the rest of these meaty delicacies—the ripest and sourest that there are, if possible. Keep back a good portion, though, for any poor devils that the bad weather might bring us. As for your friends, try to regale them as much as they like with chestnuts gilded under the embers, while washing them down liberally with sweet white wine fresh from the cask, which will soften them up nicely. When there are no more, there'll be something else . . ."

Toussaint wiped away a tear and hugged the old woman before continuing: "I wouldn't leave you all this work, beloved mother, if my dear Scholastique were still alive—but God has decided only to leave you to mother my children, and to be a visible providence for their father."

"Everything will be done as you desire, my worthy Toussaint," said the worthy Huberte, as moved as her son by the memory he had awakened with his final words. "Have a good time for the little that remains of your feast-day, for the hours are passing quickly. When the monastery bell announces the first prayers for the dead, we'll have the leisure to think about them. Enjoy yourself heartily, and don't worry about your guests. Here come two here already, Heaven be praised, whom we'll do our best to receive well, and who'll be indulgent in forgiving the paltriness of our means, if our welcome doesn't respond to our good will."

"May the Lord be with them," Toussaint said, greeting the strangers, whom he had not noticed until then, "and may they treat my home as if it were their own! Tell them some good stories to help blunt the tedium of the hours, and don't spare the provisions; in a workman's house, every day brings its bread."

Then he embraced his mother once again, and went away.

The two men of whom old Huberte had spoken had risen to their feet momentarily in response to Toussaint's politeness; then they sat down again, silently, on the far side of the fireplace.

The first of them had the appearance of a person of some distinction. He wore a black jacket with laces, over which was folded a large white ruff with generous folds, well-starched and well-fluted. His legs were encased, to a point immediately above the knee—the height to which his cloth cape also descended—by a good pair of leather gaiters, fastened on the outside. His hat, pulled down, was embellished with a floating plume, which fell down over his eyes. His pointed and graying beard only testified a robust old age, and his discreet and elegant attitude gave him the appearance of a doctor.

The other, to judge by his small stature, had to be a child of common extraction, but his extraordinary costume had immediately attracted the attention of Huberte and the young women of the dale, who regretted being unable to make out his features through the enormous clumps of red hair that covered almost the whole of his face. He was clad in a pair of breeches and an exceptionally tight crimson doublet. The top of his head was hidden by a woolen skull-cap of the same color, from which the bright blond head of hair that lent him such a strange physiognomy burst forth in crimped curls. That bonnet of sorts was fastened under the chin by a sturdy strap, like the muzzle of a vicious dog.

"You will be better able to excuse us for failing in our duty," Huberte said, resuming her conversation and addressing the older of the two strangers, "if you understand that our poor and underpopulated country does not often have the honor of being visited by travelers like you. It must have been chance that brought you here."

"Chance or the fiery furnace," replied the man in black, in a hoarse voice, the sharp tone of which startled the younger women.

"It's sometimes the same thing," the dwarf put in, leaning back and letting out an ear-splitting burst of laughter, although he contrived not to render any part of his face visible, save for an immense mouth liberally equipped with teeth that were pointed like needles and as white as ivory.

Immediately afterwards, he set his stool beside the fire-irons and extended towards the brazier two very long and emaciated hands. The flame shone right through them, as though they were made of horn.

The man in black paid no immediate attention to that brutal banter. "My damnable horse," he went on, "carried away by fear of the storm, led me astray for three hours, from one woodland to another and one ravine to another, until it finally made the decision to throw me into a precipice, where I was left for dead. I think I'd covered a good thirty leagues, and I was only guided through the unfamiliar territory by the light of your forge and the grace of God."

"His divine will be accomplished in all things," said Mother Huberte, making the sign of the cross.

"The grace of God could do nothing less," the mischievous little man put in, "to assist the most illustrious, most reverend and most noble Master Pancrace Chouquet, former instigator of the Monastery of the Daughters of Saint Columba, minister of the Holy Gospel, rector of the University of Heidelberg and doctor in four faculties."

That statement was followed by a burst of laughter even louder than the first.

"By what right," cried the doctor, grinding his teeth, "does an uncouth lout of your kind dare to involve himself in my conversation, and to attribute names and titles to me that might not be mine at all? Where have you met me before?"

"I beg your pardon, my gentle master—don't get carried away," the fellow replied, stroking the doctor's cape and sleeve with his huge hand. "I saw you in Cologne while making my tour of Europe, in order to complete my education, in accordance with the dearest wishes of my father. I attended one of the lectures in which you were translating Plutarch into excellent Latin, when you suddenly stopped, quite at a loss—as if Satan had taken you by the throat—at the treatise *De Sera Numinis Vindicta*. It's beautiful and scholarly material. It's true that you had other affairs to see to that day—a bed was being warmed up for you behind the tomb of the three kings that was even more ardent than Dame Huberte's hearth. The story is rather amusing, and I'd willingly tell it if that were the desire of this amiable and happy company."

"And I," said the doctor, in a low voice, "if you mention the matter again, will shove it back into your soul with my dagger! It's surprising," he added, growling, "that a rogue like you should be received into such an honest house."

"I took him to be your servant," Madame Huberte told him. "I don't know him otherwise."

"Nor me, nor me," said the young women, huddling together like baby birds taken from a nest.

"Me neither," said Cyprienne, hiding her head between Maguelonne's knees.

"Oh, the mischievous children!" cried the traveler in the red skull-cap, from the corner of the fireplace, where he crouched down to pull out the burning chestnuts with sharp claws. "See how naughty they are, pretending not to recognize me in my Sunday clothes! Look how much he's changed, Madame Huberte, the little neighborhood horse-trader, Colas Papelin, formerly a clerk, now a groom, at your service. Honest Master Toussaint has not applied his iron to a single one of your mares that I have not previously washed, brushed, combed, smoothed, waxed, polished, brighter than a mirror, and whose horsehair I haven't teased with my fingers at all hours—or by night, at least. That's why I'm always well received at the forge—because the ostler and the farrier, as the saying goes, have only one hand."

While delivering this speech, he moved the thick curls of his flamboyant hair to the left and the right, uncovering his face. Laughing loudly enough to shake the walls, he displayed a rather ugly countenance, as pale and jaundiced as the wax of an old candle, furrowed with bizarre wrinkles, in the front of which shone two little red eyes, brighter than coals incessantly excited by the draught of a pair of bellows. Everyone started with alarm.

Dame Huberte knew perfectly well that she had never seen him before, but a feeling deep inside warned her that it was not a good idea to say so.

"If I've ever seen this phantom before," Pancrace muttered, "he must be the great Devil of Hell."

"It could well have been there," Colas Papelin replied, still laughing, "and I would have been as astonished as you are by the hazard which has found us both here. Who would have ever expected to find Master Pancrace Chouquet in Hermit's Dale?"

"In Hermit's Dale!" said Pancrace, in a thunderous voice. "Ah! Ah!" he went on, biting his fist.

"Ah! Ah!" Colas Papelin repeated, infernal mockery in his tone. "But do you not think, as I do, Doctor, that it would be rather amusing for we men of letters, among whom the love of instruction is combined with the love of gold and pleasure, to find out why this miserable vale is so called? The story must be a singular one, and it's my opinion that Dame Huberte—who knows all the good stories in the world—will tell us that one between two jugs of sweet wine."

"I don't much care for stories, my good man," replied Pancrace, making as if to rise to his feet.

"If it isn't that one, it'll be mine," cried Colas Papelin, putting the other back in his seat, gripping him with wiry arms that squeezed him like a vice. "Oh, we'll obtain great pleasure, Dame Huberte, from hearing you tell that one."

"I promised to tell it to my daughters," the old woman replied, "and it isn't a long story. It's necessary, first, to tell you that this country was even wilder and sadder than you find it more than a hundred years ago, when a holy man came to found a little hermitage on one of the rocky ledges that border the precipice. It was said that he was a rich young lord, and that he'd removed himself from the court for fear of not being able to find salvation there, but he was never known by any other name than Odilon—under which the Holy Father has beatified him, while he awaits canonization."

"Damn!" said Colas Papelin.

"At any rate," Huberte continued, "no one had any doubt that he had brought plenty of money with him, for in less than no time the face of the dale was completely changed. He brought in laborers to till the land, constructed a water-mill on the stream, built a little hospice, a presbytery, a monastery . . . and his generosity attracted tradesmen to the dale, of every kind useful to travelers. Their families still live here, albeit in mediocre accommodation, never ceasing to glorify the name of the Blessed Saint Odilon, who appointed them his heirs. That's why this valley is called Hermit's Dale—because he never left his hermitage, and, in imitation of God, he was good to men without ever being seen. The Lord has his soul before his face, exactly as it says in the prayer-book."

"The story is very edifying," said Doctor Pancrace, "and I would like to believe it on this occasion, although I have heard its like everywhere that monks are to be found—but it seems to me that the weather is getting better again: the wind has stopped roaring and the rain is no longer battering the windows."

"It would be pleasant to resume our journey immediately," Papelin remarked, gaily, keeping the doctor in his seat, "but it would be far too impolite to abandon Dame Huberte at the beginning of such a good and instructive narrative."

"The narrative is quite complete," the doctor replied, impatiently, "and has made clear everything that we could expect from it—which is to say, the origin and the etymology of this valley's name; there is not a word lacking."

"It lacks," Colas replied, "a change of fortune, a denouement and a moral, of a kind for which we students on the benches would not have thanked you when you took the trouble to explain the arguments of Master Guillaume Fichet[1] to us. Look, if you need proof: the venerable Madame Huberte is ready to continue now that she has got her breath back."

She had indeed resumed her story. "The Blessed Odilon had lived thus, in retreat and devoted to prayer, for nearly three quarters of a century, when a young man volunteered to assist him in his holy offices, who had attracted attention for some months by the devotion of his practices and the assiduity of his sacraments. As the young man had the knowledge of a priest, the eloquence of a preacher and the apparent piety of a saint—for no one had ever seen a penitent whose mortifications were so carefully-researched—the hermitage was easily opened to him. His name escapes my memory for the moment, although it seems to me that I heard it spoken not long ago."

"The name of that person is completely irrelevant to your story," murmured the doctor, gnawing at his fingers again.

---

1 Guillaume Fichet, 1433-c. 1480, was a rector of the University of Paris, who helped to establish the first printing-press in the city.

"Master Pancrace Chouquet," Colas Papelin repeated, in a more strident tone, "thinks that the name of this person is irrelevant to your story, respectable hostess!" He went on to add, crying out even more strongly: "Hear this! Your story can do without the name of the good apostle, who seems to me to be an infernal hypocrite—such is the opinion of Messire Pancrace, Messire Chouquet, and Messire Pancrace Chouquet! So you don't recall the name, Madame Huberte?"

The wretch wants to see me dead! the doctor thought, for his part, as he turned his eyes towards the door.

"Not yet," little Colas Papelin replied to his thought, choking with laughter.

"We had feared for a long time that the lure of the Blessed One's treasure might tempt thieves," Tiphaine's widow continued, having taken scant notice of these interruptions, "but we knew by this time that after having distributed a great part in charitable works—as I have mentioned earlier—he had divided the remainder between the parish and the monastery for the education of children, the solace of travelers and the repair of storm-damage. No one in the valley saw anything in the arrival of the young cleric, therefore, but a gentle source of comfort sent by the grace of Providence to ease the last years of the hermit. At least, we said to our old people, the holy man will have someone beside him to close his eyes, and to summon the blessings of Heaven upon his head by giving him the last rites."

"Oh, that was a worthy thought, brave woman!" cried Colas Papelin, sobbing. "I swear that I would have blessed the head of that benevolent old man myself, if

God had permitted it! What says my master, Messire Pancrace Chouquet?"

Pancrace twisted his beard, shifted on his stool, looked at the door again, and made no reply.

"That's good," the old woman went on. "One night, Tiphaine sat up in bed beside me. It was thirty years ago today, on the Eve of All Saints, just before the morning mass for the dead."

"What?" said Colas Papelin. "Do you mean, my good mother, that exactly thirty years has passed since that day: that it will be thirty years to the hour, not a minute more and not a minute less, when matins sounds?"

"It must be, honest Monsieur Papelin," Huberte replied, "for it was in 1531. I asked Tiphaine what had woken him up at such an hour, thinking that he must be ill. 'Lie down,' he replied, 'and don't be afraid, old girl. It was just a bad dream, but I have to set my mind at rest before I go back to sleep, for dreams are sometimes communications from the Lord. It seemed to me that someone murdered the old holy man Odilon, and since I woke up I don't know what sort of commotion's got into me. Don't worry—I'll be back in a minute.' So saying, he ran to the hermitage with some of the workmen possessed by the same anxiety—and they found that their dreams had instructed them only too well!"

"The poor hermit was dead," said Colas. "Do you hear, Master?"

"He was dead when Tiphaine got there—but even though he must have fallen without offering the slightest sign of life to the eyes of his murderer, he had found enough strength afterwards to drag himself outside his cell, while the wretch searched fruitlessly for the imagined treasures that he would pay for with his soul!"

"And his murderer was the deceptive and detestable monster who had concealed himself within the amity and prayers that constituted his mask of devotion! Do you hear, Master?"

Pancrace's only reply was a kind of dull moan resembling the cry of an animal.

"It was him all right!" said Dame Huberte. "The grille of the cell had closed behind the Blessed One, by means of an apparatus which Tiphaine had devised, whose secret was unknown to the assassin."

"Caught at last!" cried Colas Papelin, with his usual horrible laugh. "A few moments more, and the good will be avenged. Do you hear, Master?"

"It wasn't like that," Huberte went on, shaking her head. "Tiphaine and his men found no one in the cave, and because the odor of bitumen and sulfur suddenly poured out of it, it was assumed that the stranger had made a pact with the Devil to escape the danger in which he was placed—which turned out to be the case, for we found out later that he had studied at Metz or Strasbourg under the vile sorcerer Cornelius,[1] of whom you must have heard."

"Oh, his bargain was dearly bought," Colas Papelin put in, letting out a new gale of laughter. "Do you hear, Master?"

---

1 Cornelius Agrippa (1486-1535) was a famous German philosopher, whose studies of alchemy and magic won him a belated reputation as a sorcerer that was dramatically enhanced by the false attachment of his name to a treatise on black magic.

"I hear," Pancrace Chouquet replied, in a tone of affected calm. "I hear the language of superstitious folly, with which papism has nourished these ignorant folk. May the light of truth descend upon them!" And he made a sudden movement to pull away from his companion. Colas Papelin did not attempt to detain him, but merely turned upon him an expression of derision and contempt.

"What is certain," added the old woman, slightly piqued, "is that what remained in the cave was a fragment of parchment, stained with blood and bearing the marks of five great black fingernails, like a royal seal, which guaranteed thirty years of respite to the homicide—or so it appeared, in a translation made by Monseigneur the great penitentiary, for it was written in a diabolical script."

"Either there's a ringing in my ears," murmured Colas Papelin, "or that's matins sounding. Do you hear, Master?"

"The assassin has never been seen since," Huberte concluded, "although he left a token of his presence behind: the hand of the Blessed One contained a thick handful of hair attached to a bloody piece of skin, which could not be detached from his grip."

"Good for Saint Odilon!" said Colas Papelin, rising abruptly to his feet and sending the doctor's plumed hat flying from his head with a sudden sweep of his arm.

One side of Master Pancrace Chouquet's head was bald, as glossy as if it had been seared by fire.

The doctor measured Colas with a menacing stare, gathered up his hat, and went to the door. He looked behind to see if the groom was following him, but the little man was amusing himself by using an iron poker to make the fire glow red, drawing out sparks that sprang up as far as the arched top of the fireplace.

The door closed again.

The entire group of women remained silent and motionless, weighed down by an uncanny terror, as if they had been petrified. Colas Papelin looked at them, laughing even louder. He bowed to them, brushing back his disordered hair with the coquettish grace of a man of the world educated in good manners and polite habits.

"Adieu, respectable Huberte, and to you, gentle maidens," he said, as he departed. "Thanks are due to you for the hospitality we have received, but I have other duties to perform—I must follow that gentleman along the road, lest he escape me."

An instant later, the creak of hinges was heard, and the sturdy shutters rebounded against the door.

"Is the Devil gone, then?" cried the blonde Julienne, lifting her tiny trembling hands towards Heaven.

"The Devil!" said Anastasia, putting her hands together in an attitude of prayer. "Do you think that's who he was?"

"He certainly gave the impression," Madame Huberte observed, gravely, "of someone who stopped telling his rosary beads a long time ago."

"Didn't he name himself?" Julienne replied, slightly reassured. "Colas Papelin and the Devil—it's the same thing."

"The two names are exactly synonymous," added Demoiselle Ursule—who was the niece and goddaughter of the parish priest—knowingly.

"I know where I've seen him before," said Cyprienne. "I've seen him stoking the fire in exactly that fashion, when I've fallen asleep at my distaff!"

"Me too," said Maguelonne. "I've seen him mischievously tying the tails of our goats together, when I'm on watch in the cowshed!"

"It must be him," said little Annette, the daughter of Robert the miller, suddenly, "who frightens our donkeys by whistling in the wood!"

"He wanted to scare us too," replied her sister Catherine, in a low voice. "The Evil One in the red jerkin has done more than one of his tricks on the banks of the stream in the dale."

"Deliver us, Lord!" cried old Huberte, falling to her knees.

One can well imagine that the young ladies followed her example quickly enough, and that they did not go their separate ways in response to the matins bell without having purified Dame Huberte's kitchen with prayers, the burning of incense and aspersions of holy water.

The following morning, as the people of the hamlet took themselves off to mass at the monastery, which was separated from the forge by a patch of scrubland, Toussaint Oudard suddenly quit the arm of his mother and stepped in front of his little flock, warning them with a gesture and a cry to go no further, for he wished to spare them the hideous spectacle by which his own eyes had been struck.

It was a corpse, so horribly lacerated, so contorted by the convulsions of agony, so shriveled and desiccated by the action of some celestial or infernal fire, that it would have been difficult to recognize it as human, were it not for the shreds of a black cape and a plumed hat that were trailing beside it.

And ever since that day, Hermit's Dale has been known as Dead Man's Dale.

THE DEVIL'S CHESS GAME

by S. Henry Berthoud

> Seigneurs and ladies who have heard
> good stories told,
> if it pleases you to listen and remember,
> I have a good one to tell.
> So, please pick up this little book, correcting its
> faults if you find any,
> which is newly translated from
> old rhymes and prose.
> Prologue to *Histoire de Richard-Sans-Peur*[1]

THE Sire de Clairmarais had been out hunting since the early hours. His wife, the chatelaine, was occupying the leisure of a long autumn evening in her oratory, embroidering a veil of precious golden cloth destined to ornament the miraculous reliquary of the blessed Saint

---

1 *Histoire de Richard sans Peur, duc de Normandie, fils de Robert le Diable* was a chapbook originally published by Garnier in 1736, popularizing a sequel to the popular legend of *Robert le Diable*, which became the basis of a famous opera by Giacomo Meyerbeer, première in Paris in 1831. Berthoud appended versions of both legends to his collection of *Chroniques et traditions surnaturelles de la Flandre.*

Bertin.[1] Her ladies in waiting were working around her in silence, for their mistress was too haughty to chat with vassals, and even to permit them to raise their voices in her presence except in response to her request.

An hour after the wind had ceased to bring the last chimes of the curfew rung at the belfry of Saint-Omer, a village about half a league away, to the château, the blast of a horn was suddenly heard at the manor's postern. There was something strange and wild about the fanfare that made the chatelaine and her ladies tremble. A page went to enquire as to who it was, and came back to inform his mistress that a knight of noble appearance, who called himself Sire Brudemer, was requesting hospitality.

If some poor laborer in mortal danger had been lamenting on the far side of the moat, the chatelaine would not have had the drawbridge lowered to give him shelter in the manor, but a noble lord was another matter entirely. She gave the order that he should be admitted to the château and introduced to her presence.

Then, in accordance with custom, she set about preparing with her own hands the hypocras that one had to offer guests as a gesture of welcome. She had just finished pouring the beverage into a silver cup when Sire Brudemer was brought in by the page.

He advanced toward the chatelaine with the charming and noble courtesy typical of a high-born knight, and

---

1 The ruined Benedictine abbey founded in the seventh century and dedicated to its second abbot, St. Bertin, in Saint-Omer, was one of the most famous monuments in the region that Berthoud calls Flanders. In the period when Berthoud wrote the story its stone was being plundered in order to build Saint-Omer's Hôtel-de-Ville, completed in 1834.

began by thanking the lady politely for the hospitality that she had granted him.

"I have lost my way in the domain," he said. "A little while ago I was cursing the impetuosity of my horse, which, separating me from my huntsmen, drew me into marshes and ravines and the deepest thickets; but since I have been fortunate enough to be admitted to the presence of such a marvelously beautiful lady, I no longer take any account of fatigues, danger or anxieties."

At first, the stranger's voice had something bitter and coarse about it, but that was soon forgotten thanks to the honeyed grace of his words.

The ladies in waiting, who, in accordance with custom, had retired to the far side of the room, in such a way that they could see what was happening without being able to hear anything that was said, exchanged remarks in low voices regarding the richness of Brudemer's vestments, the elegance of his bearing, the symmetry of his features and the grim expression in his fiery eyes. Thus, it was not surprising that the chatelaine found an inexpressible charm in the society of her guest. She had had no other companions than vassals since birth, and her conversations had been limited to long accounts of her aged husband's battles and tournaments, he being a better wielder of the lance than an amiable gallant.

Profiting skillfully from his advantages, Brudemer did not take long to mingle with his discourse something more flattering and more affectionate than the chivalric mores of the era permitted. The chatelaine, ordinarily so proud and disdainful, subjugated by an unknown power, listened to him without anger, and then with ever-increasing emotion.

Then, placing himself unceremoniously in such a way as to hide the Dame de Clairmarais from her ladies in waiting, he took possession of a hand that she did not think of withdrawing, and raised it tenderly to his lips; then, his knee pressed gently upon a knee that was trembling.

It would be difficult to describe the chatelaine's sensations: a harsh, infernal fire was circulating dolorously in her veins; it gripped her forehead and caused her bosom to heave. She did not experience any of the sweet languor and the ineffable intoxication that are the gentle and cruel symptoms of love-sickness; there was, instead, anguish, a cold sweat and the frissons of a sinner at fault; there was, instead, the horrible stupefaction of a pilgrim whose sees the mortal gaze of a basilisk fixed upon him.

In her disturbance, the Dame de Clairmarais dropped the veil that she was embroidering. "Oh, if I were granted the gift of such a scarf," said Brudemer, "if the lady whose beautiful hands have fashioned it took me for her knight, how many lances I would break in her honor on the tourney-field and in battle!"

She picked it up with a convulsive movement and said to him: "Here it is!"

Brudemer raised the scarf to his lips, in order to hide a horrible smile that he could not repress—but he suddenly threw it away with a frisson of terror, as if it were made of fire. The chaplain had examined it the previous evening, after vespers, with his hands still moist with holy water.

Immediately recovering from his emotion, however, he drew nearer to the chatelaine and lowered his voice to say: "I was guided to your castle by an old man in great haste to see the Sire de Clairmarais. He's waiting at the postern to tell him an important secret, which concerns you."

The chatelaine went pale at those words.

"I asked," Brudemer continued, "about the motives that caused him to seek out your husband in such a hurry. His purpose, he told me, is to reveal a mystery to him—a mystery that might well lead to changes in the manor of Clairmarais. 'The chatelaine,' he said, 'has expelled me ignominiously from the château; she has threatened to have me thrown in the moat if I return. The ingrate! I'll deprive her of her titles and her wealth, of which she is so proud.'

"As I did not want to add faith to these threats, he told me that his wife had been the nurse of the daughter of the Comte d'Érin; that the nursling had died without anyone in the world knowing it except him; that he had put you, his own daughter, in the dead young comtesse's crib, and that you had been brought up and married as the child of the Seigneur d'Érin. He furnished me with numerous and irrefutable proofs of his fraud.

"Once this mystery is known, the Sire de Clairmarais will not take long to repudiate a vassal, the daughter of an ignoble serf by whom he had been duped."

The chatelaine wrung her hands in despair.

"Listen," Brudemer continued, lowering his voice even further, but in such a manner that the Dame de Clairmarais would not miss a single word. "The old man, wrapped in his cloak, is asleep outside the postern: take this dagger . . . come . . ."

"My father!"

"No, you're right," Brudemer replied, with an ironic coldness. "Who knows? Perhaps, out of pity, you'll be admitted among the ladies in waiting of the Sire de Clairmarais' new wife. At the worst, you'll only be shaved and locked up in a convent . . ."

The chatelaine rose to her feet swiftly, made a gesture to her women forbidding them to follow her, and gave her hand to Brudemer. They both went down to the postern.

After having hunted all day, the Sire de Clairmarais came back, where he expected to find himself before long before a roaring fire, beside his wife, the beautiful chatelaine.

He was in such haste to arrive that he was preceding his huntsmen by a short distance when his horse suddenly refused to advance any further, rearing up and giving signs of great fear. The old seigneur was forced to dismount. Oh, how surprised and chagrined he was to see his wife's foster-father lying there, unmoving, with a deep wound in his breast.

People hastened around the old man, and the care that they lavished upon him had not been in vain. He opened his eyes, raised himself up effortfully, and, leaning close to the ear of the Sire de Clairmarais, murmured a few words that had made the castellan shudder with horror; then he fell back and died.

Without proffering a single word, the old seigneur marched straight to the oratory, where he found his wife.

Her forehead covered by a mortal pallor, she was sitting in front of a narrow table, and, in order to conceal her trouble, was pretending to play chess with Brudemer.

The latter, at the sight of the Sire de Clairmarais, emitted a horrible burst of laughter. The chatelaine shared that execrable hilarity, and must have been suffering a great deal to laugh like that.

Then the Sire de Clairmarais had no further doubt as to his misfortune—for until that moment, he had been unable to believe in the crimes of which the dying man had accused the chatelaine. "Satan!" he cried, at the peak of indignation and despair. "Satan! I abandon the parricide, the adulterous spouse and the château she has soiled with her presence, to you."

"I accept," said Brudemer. At the same time, a crown of flames sprang forth around his head, and he reached out for the chatelaine's white shoulders with two terrible hands that were suddenly armed with infernal claws.

It was more than two hundred years after the Sire de Clairmarais had died in an odor of sanctity in the abbey of Saint Bertin when, one evening, a monk of the order of Saint Benedict asked an inhabitant of Saint-Omer what the manor was whose towers could be seen in the middle of a wood surrounded by immense marshes.

"May Our Lady and the saints protect you!" the townsman replied. "That's the Château de Clairmarais, an accursed place haunted by the Demon. Every night, it lights up with a sudden glow; every night, the Devil and

I don't know how many revenants arrive there in their chariots of fire.

"If the old people of the region can be believed, the demon that inhabits the château is named Brudemer, and forces the insensate individuals who penetrate his abode to play chess for their souls, in exchange for the property of the domain and all the treasures it contains. As you can imagine, no one, as yet, has been able to beat the devil, and, in consequence, no one has come back from Clairmarais."

The monk listened to the townsman in silence, and then, after having reflected briefly, he marched at a firm step toward the diabolical manor.

He got in without meeting any obstacle, and went to sit down in a richly-furnished oratory, in the middle of which there was a narrow table on which a chessboard was set and all the pieces for a game.

While the monk was examining these objects, which nightfall was beginning to render indistinct, a bright light suddenly flooded the oratory and the monk was surrounded by a crowd of varlets, pages and ladies-in-waiting dressed in an antique style. All of them carried out their duties in silence, without their footsteps being audible, and, marvelously, without their bodies producing a shadow when they passed in front of the light.

Shortly afterwards, a richly-dressed seigneur advanced, who wore on his blazoned doublet, by way of an armory, a divided shield forked with sable, with the device: *Brudemer*. On his arm there was a woman, still young, whose beautiful features were covered with a cadaverous pallor; then came eight pages, bowed down beneath the weight of four heavy coffers filled with gold.

Brudemer sat down at the chessboard and made a sign to the monk inviting him to sit opposite. The monk obeyed, and they commenced playing without either of them saying a single word.

By means of clever strategy, the monk believed that he had checkmated his adversary when the pale lady, who had remained standing behind Brudemer and leaning on the back of his large armchair leaned over and pointed at a pawn. Then the game changed its aspect, and it was the monk who found himself in danger of being checkmated.

Having brought off that coup, Brudemer and the lady burst out laughing, and all the people in the oratory gathered around the players, taking part in that frightful fit of gaiety, which no human words can describe.

The monk began to regret his temerity. Cold sweat formed on his brow, and he would have given anything in the world to find himself back in his convent at that moment. Nevertheless, he did not despair of divine bounty, and he appealed mentally to his blessed patron Saint Benedict, for only a miracle could get him out of the dangerous pass. Suddenly, thanks to a celestial inspiration, he perceived that a new stratagem might yet enable him to win the game, and he was about to advance the pawn that would ensure him of it when the bursts of laughter that were resounding around him changed into frightful howls. Then he heard and saw no more.

The monk, after having spent all night in prayer, finally saw dawn break with a joy that is easily imaginable. He found, in the place occupied by the pale lady, a skeleton covered in ragged shreds of rich women's clothing.

Left the owner of the château and the wealth it contained, the monk made the accursed place into a monastery, of which he was appointed the superior. No more of it remains today that meager vestiges of the cloister, destroyed in the epoch of the Revolution.

How I regret not having been able to recount the story in the native dialect and with the expression of credulity of the old woman who told it to me, in a poor cottage lit by a single lamp and the red glow of the hearth, while the rain fell in torrents and the roaring wind plunged into the immense wood of Clairmarais.[1]

---

1 In fact, the village of Clairmarais, near Saint-Omer, owes its name not to some Feudal overlord of that name but to a Latin improvisation by Saint Bernard, the founder of the Cistercian abbey that was established in the marsh in 1140. The last vestiges of the abbey are still visible, but it was destroyed during the Revolution, in 1790, when Clairmarais became a commune.

A DREAM OF HELL

by Gustave Flaubert

I

THE earth was dormant in a lethargic slumber, no noise at its surface, and nothing could be heard but the waters of the ocean breaking into foam on the rocks. The owl made its cry heard in the cypresses, the drooling lizard dragged itself over the tombs, and the vulture came to alight on the rotten bones on the battlefield,

A heavy and abundant rain obscured the dubious light of the moon, before which the gray clouds passing across the azure flowed, flowed and flowed again.

The wind of the tempest agitated the waves and made the leaves of the forest tremble; it whistled in the air, sometimes strong and sometimes weak, like a shrill screech dominating the murmurs.

And a voice emerged from the earth and said: "End the world! Let its last hour be today!"

"No, no; it's necessary that all the hours sound."

"Hasten them," said the first voice. "Exterminate humankind in a seventh chaos, and don't create any other worlds."

"There will be another one superior to this."

"More wretched, you mean," replied the voice of the earth. "Oh, finish, for the good of your creatures; since all your works thus far have failed, at least don't make any more."

"Yes, yes," replied the voice of heaven, "the other humankinds have complained of their weakness and their passions; this one will be strong and devoid of passions. As for the soul . . ."

Here the voice of the earth started laughing: a loud laughter that filled the abyss with its immense disdain.

II

Duc Arthur d'Almeroës was an alchemist, or was at least reputed to be such, although his servants had remarked that he rarely worked, that his furnaces were always ashes and never braziers, and that the pages of his opened books were never turned; nevertheless, he spent days, nights and entire months without emerging from his laboratory, plunged in profound meditations, like a man who is working and thinking. It was thought that he was in search of gold, the elixir of long life, and the philosopher's stone. He was, therefore, a very cold man externally, very deceptive in appearance: never a smile of wellbeing on his lips, nor a word of anguish, never a cry in his mouth; no feverish and ardent nights such as men have who dream of something great. One might have thought him, on seeing him thus, serious and cold, an automaton who thought like a man.

The people—for it is necessary to cite everywhere that which has become the mightiest of powers and the most holy of things; two terms that seem incompatible except with reference to God: sanctity and power—were therefore convinced that he was a sorcerer, a demon, Satan incarnate. He it was who laughed, in the evening, in the corner of the cemetery, who trailed slowly over the cliff uttering cries like an owl; he it was who was seen dancing in the fields with the fire follets; he it was whose somber and lugubrious face was seen floating over the old feudal keep, like an old bloody legend over the ruins of a tomb.

Often, in the evening, when the peasants seated outside their doors rested from their day's work, singing some old song of the region, some old national song that their fathers had learned from their grandfathers and they had transmitted to their own children, which they had learned in their childhood and sung in their youth on the mountain where they took their goats to pasture, then, at that hour of repose when the moon begins to appear, when the bats flutter unevenly around the bell-tower, when the crow settles of the strand in the pale radiance of a dying sun, at that moment, I say, Duc Arthur was sometimes seen to appear.

And then people fell silent, when the sound of his footfalls was heard; children huddled close to their mothers and men looked at him with astonishment; they were frightened of that leaden gaze, that cold smile and that pale face, and if anyone touched his hands, they found them as glacial as a reptile's skin.

He passed quickly through the peasants, silenced by his approach, disappeared promptly and was lost to sight, as rapid as a gazelle, as subtle as a fantastic dream or a shade, and gradually the sound of his footfalls and the dust diminished, and no trace of his passage remained behind him, except for the dread and the terror, like a pallor after a storm.

If anyone had been bold enough to follow him in his winged course, to see where that course was heading, they would have seen him enter the old ruined keep, which no one dared approach in the evening, for strange noises were heard there that faded away in the loopholes of the towers, and by night a great black phantom regularly walked, which extended its long arms toward the clouds, and whose bony hands caused the stones of the castle to tremble, with the rattle of chains and the gasps of a dying man.

Well, that man who appeared so infernal and so terrible, who seemed to be a child of Hell, the thought of a demon, the work of a damned alchemist, whose cracked lips seemed only to dilate at the touch of fresh blood, whose white teeth exhaled an odor of human flesh, that infernal being, that deadly vampire, was merely a pure and intact intelligence, as cold and perfect, as infinite and regular, as a marble statue that could think and act, which had a will, a power—a soul, in sum—but whose blood did not beat warmly in his veins, who had understanding without feeling, an arm without a thought, eyes without passion and a heart without amour.

Away with all need for life, all material reality!—everything for thought, for ecstasy, but a vague and indefinite ecstasy that bathes in the clouds, that is mirrored in the moon, and holds instinct and constitution like the perfume in a flower.

His face was handsome, his gaze fine; his hair was long, and undulated marvelously over his shoulders in long azure waves when he bent down and folded himself over his elongated back, the skin of which, silvered by a reflection of the snow, was as soft as satin and as white as the moon.

The other creatures before him had had passions, a body, a soul, and they had all acted pell-mell in some turbulence, rushing upon one another, pushing and pulling; some of them had been elevated, others trampled underfoot; all the other humans, in sum, had been pressed, heaped up and stirred in that immense crowd, in that long cry of anguish, in the prodigious quagmire called life.

But he, a celestial spirit, cast upon the earth as the last word of creation, a strange and singular being, arrived in the midst of humans without being a human like them, having their willful body, their form, their speech, their gaze, but of a superior nature, with a more elevated heart, which only required passions to nourish itself, and which, seeking them on earth in accordance with its instinct, had found nothing but humans. What, then, was he to do? He was shrunk, worn and bruised by our customs and our instincts.

Would he, who had only ever had the appearance of flesh, have understood our carnal pleasures? The warm embraces of a woman, her arms moist with sweat, her tears of amour, her breasts bare—would all of that have made him, who had found in the depths of his heart an infinite science and an immense world, palpitate one morning?

Our poor sensuality, our paltry poetry, all of the earth, with its joys and its delights—what had he, who had something of the angels, made of all that? So he suffered ennui on that earth, but the ennui that eats away like a cancer, which burns you, which lacerates you, and ends in humans with suicide. But him, suicide? Oh, how many times he was glimpsed, up on the high cliff, gazing at the death that was there before him with a bitter laugh, laughing in its face and mocking it with the emptiness of the space that refused to swallow him!

How many times he had contemplated at length the mouth of a pistol, and then thrown it away with rage, unable to make use of it, because he was condemned to live! Oh, how many times he spent entire nights walking in the woods, hearing the sound of the waves on the beach, scenting the odor of wrack blackening on the rocks! How many nights he spent leaning on a rock and wandering in the immensity of his thoughts, which were flying among the clouds!

But all that nature—the sea, the woods, the sky—all of that was petty and wretched; flowers had no scent on his lips; naked women were devoid of beauty for him, songs devoid of melody, the sea devoid of terror.

He did not have enough air for his lungs, not enough light for his eyes or love for his heart.

Ambition? A throne? Glory? He never thought of them. Science? Past times? But he knew the future, and in that future he had found only one thing that made him smile from time to time, while passing a cemetery.

Could he fear God, the man who felt almost his equal and who knew that a day would also come when nothingness would carry that God away, as that God would one day carry him away. Could he love him, having spent so many centuries cursing him?

Poor heart, how you suffered, embarrassed, displaced from your sphere and restricted in a world like the soul in the body! Often, an instinct mocking in itself brought a cup to his lips, the wine brushed them without a smile coming to dilate them, and then he perceived that he had done something insipid and futile; he picked a rose and withdrew from it quickly, like a thorn. One day, he wanted to be a musician; he had a sublime, strange, fantastic idea that humans might not have understood, but for which Mozart would have damned himself: an idea of genius, an infernal idea, something sickening, irritating and mortal. He began, the bewildered members of the audience stamped their feet and shouted enthusiastically, and then, mute and trembling knelt down on the flagstones and listened. Pure and plaintive sounds rose up in the nave and faded away in the vaults; it was sublime, but it was only a prelude. He wanted to continue, but the organ broke in his hands.

Nothing for him henceforth! Everything was empty and hollow; nothing but an immense ennui, a terrible solitude, and then centuries more to live, to curse existence: that man who had, however, no needs, no passions and no desires. But he had despair!

III

He resigned himself, and his superior nature gave him the means; he went to live alone and isolated in a German village, far from the abode of the humans who were his burden.

A ruined castle situated on a high hill appeared to him to be an abode in conformity with his thought, and he moved into it that evening.

He lived alone, therefore, with no retinue, no carriages, almost without servants, enclosed in himself, limiting his society to himself; his name only acquired therefrom an increasingly problematic existence. The people who served him did not know the sound of his voice, they only knew the gaze of his dull, half-closed eyes, which he turned to them coldly, making them shiver; otherwise, they were entirely free—which is to say that their master did not reproach them, and hardly ever gave them orders.

The castle in which the Duc lived had, at length, taken on something of the sadness of its residents; the blackened walls, the stones devoid of cement, the brambles that surrounded them, and the silent aspect suspended over its towers all had something magical and strange about them. It was worse inside: long obscure corridors, doors that banged violently by night and trembled in their frames, high and narrow windows, smoke-stained paneling, and then, at intervals in the galleries, some antique ornament, the armor of an ancient baron, the full-length portrait of a princess, a stag's antlers, a hunting-knife, a rusty dagger, and often, in some lightless corners, rubble, plaster fallen from the ceilings of the old drawing room when the wind, on some winter evening, intoned in the long galleries with more than customary fury and more prolonged roars.

The concierge—he was an old man as decrepit as the castle—made his round every day in the afternoon; he began with the great stone stairway whose banister had been removed since the last owner had sold it for an arpent of land; he climbed it slowly and, having arrived in the principal gallery, he opened all the rooms, all bearing their ancient numbers, all empty and dilapidated, after having once had their destination and employment.

The old drawing room was there, an immense square apartment in which one could still make out a few shreds of crimson velvet, which had formed a sumptuous ornamentation and a fresh beauty in the last century; first there was the cloakroom; then the chapel, then the drawing room. Now it was encumbered by a hundred bales of hay, deposited in that place for some twenty years, which rotted in the rain that easily penetrated through the window-panes, driven by the evening wind; the rest of the drawing room was occupied by old armchairs, worm harness, a few worm-eaten saddles and a large quantity of faggots and dry wood. The concierge never opened it except to put something old and broken into it, which he threw negligently on to some old painting, garden statue or one of the threadbare armchairs.

He resumed his slow and painful course in the middle of the corridor, and made the sound of his hob-nailed shoes resound on the stone floor-tiles, which retained their imprint; then he retraced his steps, looked at the nests of the swallows that were establishing themselves day by day in the castle, as if in their domain, and which flew back and forth through the windows of the corridor, all of whose panes were lying on the ground, broken and pell-mell with their leaden frames.

Great poplars bordered the castle; they often curbed under the breath of the ocean, the noise of whose waves mingled with that of their foliage, and their bark had been burned by the bitter air. A gap in the foliage permitted the sight, from the highest windows, of the sea that extended, immense and terrible, before the sinister castle, which seemed to be nothing but a lugubrious appanage.

Here was the drawbridge, which was now by-passed on a terrace, and there the battlements, but they trembled under the hand, and at the slightest shock the stones fell; higher up was the keep, but the concierge never went there, for he had abandoned it, along with the upper floors, to the bats and the owls that flew over the roofs by night, with their lugubrious cries and their long wing-beats.

The walls of the castle were cracked and covered with moss, and there was something damp and greasy about their contact, which oppressed the chest and caused a shiver; one might have thought it the sticky trail of a reptile.

It was there that he lived. He liked the long extended vaults, where nothing was heard but the night-birds and the wind from the sea; he liked that debris, sustained by ivy, those somber corridors, and that whole appearance of death and ruination; he, who had fallen from so high to descend so low, liked things that had also fallen; he, who was disillusioned, wanted ruins; he had found nothingness in eternity, and wanted destruction in time. He was alone in the midst of humans; he wanted to be entirely apart from them and at least to live a life that might resemble what he dreamed, what he ought to have been.

IV

Duc Arthur was sitting in a large black morocco armchair, his elbow leaning on his table, his head in his hands. The chamber he inhabited was large and spacious, its ceiling blackened by smoke; as for the paneling, it was hidden by an immense quantity of earthen pots, alembics, jars, set squares and instruments arranged on shelves.

In one corner was the furnace, with the crucible for magical operations; then, here and there, on still-warm ashes, a few open books, some pages of which had been half-torn out and seemed to have been touched by a feverish and burning hand, scanned with an avid gaze that had read nothing therein.

No light illuminated the apartment, and only a few embers that were dying in the furnace cast a glow upon the ceiling, describing vacillating luminous circles.

The alchemist remained for a long time in his motionless position; finally, he stood up, went to his crucible and considered it for a long time. The ruddy light of the embers suddenly lit up his face, coloring it with a fantastic gleam. That was surely one of the pale faces of the infernal alchemists, his eyes hollow and red, his skin white and drawn, his hands thin and elongated—all of that clearly indicated sleepless nights, burning dreams and thoughts of genius.

And you think that smile of bitterness is a smile of vanity? You think those hollow cheeks have been thinned over books, that his complexion has been bleached by the heat of fire, and that he, who would now be weeping with rage if he were a human, is in search of a name, an immortality? You think that those books thrown down with anger, those torn pages and that hand which clenches and tears, you think that he is so desperate for not having found a particle of gold, or a poison the creates life?

He was about to return to his place when he perceived, on the blackened wall, brilliant lines that stood out strongly and which soon formed a hideous and singular monster, similar to the animals that we see on the porticos of our cathedrals, famished, hollow-flanked, with the head of a dog, dugs hanging down to the ground, red fur, eyes that blazed and the spurs of a cock.

It suddenly detached itself from the wall and came to leap on to the furnace; the sound of its slender and fine paws was audible on the tiles of the crucible.

"What do you want with me?" it said to Arthur.

"Me? Nothing! But are you not the damned spirit that dooms men, and tortures their souls?"

"Well, yes," replied the monster, with an exclamation of joy. "I'm Satan."

"What do you want with me? Why have you come here?"

"To help you."

"To do what?"

"To find what you seek—gold, the elixir."

"Really! You don't know, then, that I can vivify worlds, that one thought of my head can make gold drop at my feet? No, Satan, if you only have power over that, go away, leave me alone, flee, for you can't be useful to me."

"No, no, I'll stay," said Satan, with a singular smile, "I'll stay." *Vanity is my elder daughter, she gives me the souls of all those who take her*, he thought, internally, *I'll have his soul!*

At that moment, the dying embers threw out a few more glimmers of light, which passed over Arthur's face; it appeared to Satan more beautiful and more terrible than that of the damned, and even more splendid.

"Come on, let's get out of here," Arthur said to him. "The wind's agitating the trees, the sea is growling and the shore is devastated. Come! We'll talk better about eternity and nothingness to the sound of the tempest, before the wrath of the ocean."

They went out.

The path that led to the shore was stony and shaded by the great black trees that surrounded the castle. It was cold; the ground was dry and hard; it was dark, not a star in the sky, not a ray of moonlight.

Arthur marched, bare-headed and his face uncovered; he went slowly, and took pleasure in sensing his face brushed by his blue and silky hair. He loved the racket of the wind and the sinister noise of the trees, bent over violently. Satan was behind the Duc; he leapt lightly over the stones; his head was lowered, and he was howling plaintively.

Finally, they arrived on the beach; the sand there was fresh and damp, covered with seashells and wrack, which flowed toward the sea with the pebbles dragged by the ebb-tide. They both stopped.

Arthur laughed savagely at the noise of the waves.

"This is what I love," he said, "or, rather, what I hate the least—but this anger isn't brutal enough, divine enough. Why does the tide stop, and cease rising? Oh, if the sea extended beyond the shore and the rocks, how far it would go, how it would run, how it would bound! It would be a pleasure to see, but that . . ."

"You want death, then," said Satan—"death in everything?"

"It's nothingness that I implore."

"Why? You believe, then, that nothing subsists after the body? That the closed eye sees no more, and that the cold, pale head has no more thought?"

"Yes, I believe that—for myself, at least."

"And what do you want, in sum? What do you desire?"

"Happiness!"

"Happiness? You think of that? Happiness! You'd have that in science, in glory, in amour."

"Oh, nowhere! I've searched for it for a long time, but I've never found it. Science is too limited, glory too narrow, amour too paltry."

"You believe yourself to be superior to other men, then? You believe that your soul . . ."

"Oh, my soul . . . my soul . . . !"

"You don't have one, then? You don't believe in anything . . . not even God? Oh, you'll succumb, weak and vain man, you'll succumb, for you've refused my offers; you'll succumb like the first man. How proud his gaze was, how insolent and mighty in his happiness he was, when, strolling in Eden, he contemplated my defeat with a wide and surprised eye! And he too I saw succumb; I saw him crawl at my feet, I saw him weep like me, curse and blaspheme like me; our cries of despair mingled, and from then on we were companions in torture and agony. Oh yes, you'll fall, like him, you'll love something."

"Do you take me for a human, Satan? For one of those common and vulgar creatures who crouch down on this world where a wind of misfortune has cast me into its dementia, and where I'm dying for lack of air to breathe, for lack of things to feel, to understand and to love? You believe that this mouth eats, that these teeth chew, that I'm enslaved to life like a face in a mask? If I uncovered this skin that covers me, you'd see that I too, Satan, am one of those damned beings like you, that I'm your equal and perhaps your master. Can you stop a wave, Satan? Can you knead a stone between your hands?"

"Yes."

"Satan, if I wished, I could also crush you between my hands. What do you have that renders you superior to everyone? What do you have? Is it your body? Put your head on the level of my knee or my foot, and I will crush it on the ground. What do you have that makes your glory and your pride—pride, that essence of superior spirits? What do you have? Reply!"

"My soul."

"And how many minutes in eternity can you count when that soul has given you happiness?"

"However, when I see the souls of humans suffering like mine, it's then a consolation for my dolors, a joy for my despair—but you, what do you have so divine, then? Is it your soul?"

"No; it's because I don't have one."

"No soul? What! It's an automaton, then, vivified by a flash of genius?"

"Genius! Oh, genius! Derision and pity! Me, genius? Ha!"

"No soul? And who told you that?"

"Who told me? I divined it. Listen, and you'll see. When I came to this earth, it was night: a night like this one, cold and terrible. I remember having been brought to the shore by the waves. I got up and I walked. I felt happy then, breathing freely; I had something pure and intact in the depths of my being, which made me dream and think about confused, vague, indeterminate ideas; I had a kind of distant memory of another situation, a milder and more tranquil state.

"It seemed to me, when I closed my eyes and listened to the sea, that I returned to those superior regions where all was poetry, silence and amour, and I thought I had slept continuously. That slumber was heavy and stupid, but it was pleasant and profound. In fact, I remember that there was an instant when everything passed behind me and evaporated like a dream.

"I returned from a state of intoxication and happiness to life and ennui; gradually, the dreams that I thought to recover on earth disappeared like that dream; this heart shrank, and nature appeared to me aborted, used up and old, like a counterfeit child that has the wrinkles of old age.

"I tried to imitate humans, to have their passions, their interests, to act like them; it was in vain, like an eagle wanting to hide in the nest of a woodpecker. Then everything darkened in my sight, and was nothing more than a long black veil, existence a long agony and the earth a sepulcher in which everything was buried alive.

"When, after many centuries, many ages, after having seen races of humans and empires pass before me, I felt nothing palpitating within me; when everything in my mind was dead and paralyzed, I said to myself: 'Insensate, you who want happiness and have no soul! Insensate, you who have a mind too high, a heart too elevated, you who comprehend your nothingness, who comprehend everything, who loves nothing, who believes that the body renders happiness and that matter gives happiness!' This mind, it is true, was elevated, this body was handsome, this matter was sublime, but no soul, no belief, no hope!"

"And you're complaining!" Satan said to him, dragging his dugs over the sand and extending all his length. "You're complaining! Fortunate man, on the contrary, bless heaven: you'll die! You don't desire anything, Arthur, you don't love anything; you live happily, for you resemble a stone, you resemble nothingness. Oh, what are you complaining about? What causes you chagrin? What is overwhelming you?"

"Ennui."

"Can your body not, however, procure human pleasures?"

"Human sensualities, you mean? Their great kisses, their lukewarm embraces? Oh, I've never tasted them. I disdain and scorn them."

"But a woman?"

"A woman? Oh, I'd choke her in my arms, I'd crush her with my kisses, I'd kill her with my breath. Oh, I don't have anything, you're right, I don't want anything, I don't love anything and I don't desire anything. And you, Satan, you'd like my body, wouldn't you?"

"A body? Oh yes something palpable, which feels, which sees, for I only have a form, an appearance. Oh, if I were a man! If I had a broad chest and strong thighs . . . so I envy them, I hate them, I'm jealous of them. Oh, but I only have a soul: the soul, the burning and sterile breath that devours and lacerates itself; the soul! But I can't do anything, can only skim kisses, scent and see, but I can't touch, I can't grasp. I have nothing, nothing; I only have a soul.

"Oh, how many times I've dragged myself over the cadavers of young women, still soft and warm! How many times I've returned to them, desperate and blaspheming! Why am I not a brute, an animal, a reptile? At least he has his joys, his happiness, his family; his desires are accomplished, his passions are calmed.

"You want a soul, Arthur? A soul! But have you really thought about it? Do you want to be like humans? Do you want to weep for the death of a wife, for a lost fortune? Do you want to shrivel in despair, fall from illusions to reality? A soul! Do you want cries of stupid despair, folly, idiocy? A soul! You want to believe, then? You would lower yourself to hope? A soul! You want to be human, then, a little more than a tree, a little less than a dog?"

"Well, no," said Arthur, advancing into the sea. "No, I don't want anything."

Then he fell silent, and Satan soon saw him running over the waves; his course was light and rapid, and the waves scintillated beneath his steps.

Oh, said Satan to himself, *fortunate, fortunate . . . you have ennui on the earth, but you'll sleep later, but me, me . . . I'll have despair in eternity, and when I contemplate your cadaver . . .*

"My cadaver?" said Arthur. "Who has told you that I'll die? Have I not said it? I hope for nothing, not even death."

"The most terrible means . . ."

"Try," said Arthur, who had paused momentarily on a wave on which he was bobbing gently, as if he were standing on a plank.

Satan remained silent for some time, and thought about the alchemist.

I've deceived him, he said to himself. *He doesn't believe in his soul. Oh, you'll love! You'll love a woman . . . but to that one I'll give so much grace, so much beauty, so much amour that he'll love her . . . for he's human, in spite of his pride and his science.*

"Listen, Arthur," he said, "tomorrow you'll see a daughter of the mountains, and you'll love her."

Arthur started to laugh. "Poor fool," he said. "I'd like to try, or rather for you to try, to kill me, if you dare!"

"No," said Satan, "I only have power over souls."

And he went away.

Arthur remained on the rocks, and when the moon began to appear, he opened his immense green wings, and flew away toward the clouds.

V

It was evening, and the ruddy, dying sun scarcely illuminated the valley and the mountains. It was the hour of dusk when one sees, in the meadows, white threads that attach themselves to the hair of women and garments made of lace and silky fabrics; it was the hour when the cricket sings its shrill cry in the grass and beneath the wheat. Then one hears mysterious voices in the fields, strange concerts, and then, far, far away, the sound of a little bell that calms down and diminishes, with the flocks that disappear and descend.

At that hour, the girl who looks after the goats and the cows hastens her pace, runs without looking behind her, and then stops from time to time, breathless and tremulous, for night is about to fall, and one encounters a number of men, some young, on the path, and she is sixteen, the poor child, and is afraid, so Julietta gathers her cows and heads toward the village, a few cottages of which can be made out.

That day, however, she was sad, she no longer ran to pick flowers and put them in her hair. No, no more childish leaps at the sight of a beautiful daisy that her foot was about to crush, no more joyful songs, that day, no more of those pearly notes, those long trills. No, no more joy or intoxication, no more of that pretty white neck that curved backwards, and from which a light music emerged, dancing and warm with harmony, but, on the contrary, repeated sighs, a dreamy expression, tears in the eyes, and a long walk, very pensive and very slow, in the midst of the grass, without paying attention to whether she is marching in the dew and whether her cows have disappeared, she is so nonchalant and utterly melancholy.

How many times, during the day, she ran after her herd. How many times she came back to sit down, weary and bored, and there, to think—or rather, not to think about anything! She was oppressed; her heart was burning; it desired something vague and indeterminate; it attached itself to everything, quit everything; it suffered ennui, desire and uncertainty. Ennui, dreams of the past and dreams of the future all passed through the child's head as she lay on the grass, gazing at the sky with her hands on her forehead.

She was afraid of being alone like that in the midst of the fields, and yet she had spent her childhood there, playing in the woods and running through the crops; the sound of foliage made her tremble, she dared not turn around, she always seemed to see behind her head the face of some demon grimacing with horrible laughter.

She gazed for a long time at the ruddy radiance of the sun, which was diminishing further and further, and which described, in places, luminous circles that grew, disappeared, then soon returned. She waited until the church clock had finished chiming, and when the last vibrations had died away in the distance, she got up painfully, ran after her herd, and started walking to return to her father's house.

Suddenly, fifty paces away, she saw twenty little flames that rose up from the ground. The flames disappeared, but after a few minutes, Julietta saw them again;

they drew closer and closer, and then one disappeared, then another, a third, and finally, the last, which leapt, stretched and danced with vivacity and madness.

The cows suddenly stopped, as if a natural instinct prescribed that they should go no further, and gave voice to a plaintive bellowing that went on for a long time monotonously, and then slowly died away.

The flames were redoubled, and bursts of laughter and infantile voices were clearly audible. Julietta went pale, and supported herself on the horn of a heifer, motionless and mute with terror. She heard footsteps behind her head, she felt her cheeks brushed by a hot breath, and a man came to place himself in front of her.

He was richly dressed; his garments were black silk; diamonds glittered on his gloved hand. At the slightest of his movements the silvery tinkle of bells was heard, like the stirring of gold coins. His face was ugly; his moustache was red, his cheeks hollow, but his eyes were shining like two embers; they sparkled beneath a thick and bushy brow like a fistful of hair. His forehead was pale, wrinkled and bony, and the upper fraction of it was covered by a red velvet cap. One might have thought that he was afraid of showing his head.

"Child," he said to Julietta, "beautiful child!" And he drew her toward him with a powerful hand, with a smile that he attempted to make soft, but which was only horrible. "Do you love someone?"

"Oh, leave me alone," said the young woman. "I'm dying in your arms! You're crushing me!"

"What, no one?" the knight continued. "Oh, you'll love someone, for I'm powerful—I give hate and love. Look, let's sit here, on the back of your white cow."

The cow lay down on her side and lent her flank. The stranger sat down on her back, holding one of her horns in one hand, with the other around Julietta's waist.

The fire follets had stopped. The sun was no longer illuminating; it was almost dark, and the moon, pale and weak, was struggling with the daylight.

Julietta looked at the stranger with terror; his gaze was terrible.

"Leave me alone!" she said to him. "Leave me alone, in God's name!"

"God?" he replied, bitterly, and he started to laugh. "Julietta," he went on, "do you know Duc Arthur d'Almaroës?"

"I've seen him sometimes, but he's like you; I'm afraid of him. Oh, leave me alone, leave me alone; I have to go ... my father ... oh, if he knew ..."

"Your father! Well?"

"If he knew, I tell you, that you were keeping me like this, at dusk ... oh, but he'd kill you!"

"I'll let you go, Julietta. Go."

And he dropped the arm that was gripping her firmly.

She could not get up; something attached her to the belly of the animal, which was moaning sadly and moistening the grass with its drooling tongue; it was gasping and shifting its head on the ground as if it were dying in pain.

"Well, Julietta, go! What's stopping you?"

She tried again, but nothing could enable her to make a movement; her iron will broke before the fascination of the man and his magical power.

"What's the matter with you, then?" he said to her. "What harm have I done you?"

"None . . ."

"Let's talk about Duc Arthur d'Almaroës. Isn't he rich, and handsome?" At that point he struck his forehead with both hands. "Oh, let him come! Let him come!"

Then they stayed there like that, the two of them, for a long time—a very long time—the young woman trembling, while he had his eyes fixed upon her, contemplating her avidly.

"Are you happy?" he asked her.

"Happy? Oh, no!"

"What do you need?"

"I don't know, but I don't like anything; nothing pleases me, especially today; I'm very sad, and this evening . . . your malevolent expression . . . oh, I shall go mad!"

"Isn't it the case, Julietta, that you'd like to be a queen?"

"No."

"Isn't it the case, Julietta, that you like the church and its incense, its high nave, its blackened walls and its mystical chants?"

"No."

"You like the sea, the shells on the shore, the moon in the sky and dreams at night?"

"Oh yes, I like all that."

"And what do you dream, at night?"

"How do I know?" And she became very pensive.

"Isn't it the case that you want another life, distant voyages? Isn't it the case that you'd like to be a rose leaf to roll in the air, to be the bird that flies, the song that dies away, the cry that launches forth? Isn't it the case that Duc Arthur is handsome, rich and powerful? And he too likes dreams, sublime ecstasies . . . Oh, let him come!" he continued, in a whisper. "Let him come, let him come! He'll love her, with an ardent, burning, entire amour, and they'll both be doomed."

The moon emerged from the clouds; it illuminated the mountain, the valley and the old Gothic castle, the somber silhouette of which was outlined in the moonlight like a phantom over the wall of the cemetery.

"Let's get up," said the stranger, "and walk."

The stranger took Julietta and drew her along. The cows bounded away, galloped in the fields, ran after one another, bewildered, then came back around Julietta, leaping and dancing; nothing could be heard but the sound of their feet on the ground and the voice of the cavalier with golden spurs, who was talking, always talking, with a sound as regular as an organ.

They walked like that for a long time; the path was easy, and they walked rapidly over the fresh grass, which slid underfoot like polished glass. Julietta was weary; her legs were buckling beneath her body.

"When will he arrive," she asked, often.

And her melancholy gaze launched toward the horizon, which offered her nothing but a profound obscurity.

Finally, after a very long time, she recognized her father's dwelling. The stranger was still by her side; he was no longer talking, but his face was cheerful and he was smiling like a happy man; a few words in an unknown language escaped his lips, and then he cocked an ear attentively, silent, with his mouth open.

"Do you like Duc Arthur?" he asked, one more time.

"I scarcely know him—and anyway, what does it matter to you?"

"Look there he is!" he said.

In fact, a man passed in front of them. He was naked to the waist; his body was as white as snow; his hair was blue and his eyes had a celestial gleam.

The stranger disappeared immediately.

Julietta started to run, and then, having arrived at a wooden door surrounded by a hedge, she grabbed the iron knocker and hammered forcefully. An old man came to open it; it was her father.

"Poor child," he said, "where have you been? Come in."

And the young woman immediately ran into the house, where her family had been waiting for several hours in anguish. Everyone uttered cries of joy; they embraced her, they questioned her, and they sat down at table around an enormous iron pot from which a thick vapor was exhaled.

"Have you brought the cows back?" asked her mother—and on her affirmative response she told her to go and milk them. Julietta went out, and came back after a few minutes carrying an enormous tin-plate bucket, which she deposited, with difficulty, on the table . . . but it contained blood.

"Heavens! Blood!" cried Julietta." She went pale and fell on her mother's knees. "Oh, it's him!"

"Who?"

"Him—the one who made me late."

"Who is he?"

"I don't know."

"It's me," cried a voice, coming from the depths of the apartment, with a piercing laugh.

In fact, the stranger and Duc Arthur were standing against the wall.

The old man leapt upon his rifle, hanging over the fireplace, and took aim at them.

"Have mercy on him!" cried Julietta, and threw her arms violently around his neck.

But the bullet had been fired, and nothing more could be heard. The two phantoms disappeared. After a few moments, however, a window broke and a bullet came to land on the paving-stones.

It was the one that Satan had returned.

VI

All that was strange; there was some sorcery beneath it, some magical trap. Then again, the milk changed into blood, the bizarre apparition, Julietta's lateness, her fearful gaze, her quavering voice, and the bullet that had just rebounded around them, with the sinister laughter escaping from the wall—all that made the family go pale and tremble. They huddled together and immediately fell silent.

Julietta supported her head in her left hand, placed her elbow on the table, and undid the ribbon that retained her hair; she let the tresses fall over her shoulders;

then, opening her lips, she started to sing between her teeth—very quietly, to be sure; she murmured an old refrain, bitter and monotonous, which emerged whistling. She was swaying gently in the chair and seemed to want to go to sleep to the sound of her voice; her gaze was insignificant and half-closed; her pose was nonchalant and pensive.

They listened to her with astonishment, and it was always the same sounds, shrill and faint, the same hum; but gradually, it calmed down, and became so faint and thin that it died between her teeth.

The night passed thus, sad and long, for no one dared move from their place, dared to say a word, or look behind them. The old man sighed profoundly in his wooden armchair; his wife soon closed her eyes, in dread and ennui; as for the two sons, they put their heads in their hands and sought a sleep that only came late, and was troubled by sinister dreams.

It would have been necessary to see all those slumbering and oppressed heads, gathered around a dying light that that illuminated their anxious faces with a pale and lugubrious tint. The old man's was grave; his lips were parted. His forehead was covered by white hair, and his fleshless hands rested on his thighs. The old woman, who was in front of him, turned her head from time to time to one side or the other, her face wrinkled by a singular expression of woe and bitterness. Then there was the pale and placid face of Julietta, with her long blonde hair sweeping the table, her monotonous song whistling between her white teeth, and her soft, intoxicated gaze.

She was not asleep, but she spent the hours of the night listening to the plaintive lowing of her white cow, which, enclosed in its stable, was also suffering, poor beast, perhaps writhing in agony on its litter, damp with sweat.

In fact, when day came and Julietta went out to take it to pasture in the fields, it bore the imprint of a claw on its neck.

She went out, climbed the hill at a rapid pace, arrived at the top, and sat down—but the bottom of her garments and her feet were soaking; she had walked through the dew that day, so crazy and drowsy was she, both at the same time. She ran, and then suddenly stopped, put her hand to her brow, and looked in all directions to see whether he might be coming.

Him! For she was in love, poor child. She loved a great lord, rich and powerful, who was a handsome cavalier, had proud eyes and an arrogant smile; she loved a strange, unknown man, a demon incarnate: a creature, she thought, well brought up and very poetic.

No! None of that, because she loved Duc Arthur d'Almaroës.

At other times, she fell back into her reveries and smiled bitterly, as if doubting the future, and then she thought about him, she created him for herself, there, sitting on the pearly grass beside her; he was there, there, speaking softly to her, staring at her with his powerful gaze; and his voice was soft, was pure, was vibrant with amour; it was an entirely new music, entirely sublime. She remained thus for a long time, her eyes fixed on the horizon, which always seemed to her as bleak, as empty of meaning, as stupid.

Evening finally arrived, after that long day of anguish, as long as the night that had preceded it. Julietta stayed for a long time after sunset, and then went back, descending the mountain slowly, stopping frequently and listening behind her, but she heard nothing except the cricket whistling under the grass, and the hawk going back to its nest, flapping its wings.

So she went like that, sad and desperate, her head bowed over her breast, swollen by sighs, holding in her left hand the damp rope that led her poor white cow, which was lame in its right shoulder; it was on that one that Satan had sat.

When she arrived at the place where the stranger had quit her the day before, and where Duc Arthur had appeared to her, she stopped instinctively, holding on forcefully to her heifer, which, naturally struggling against her, dragged her a few paces further.

Arthur immediately appeared; she let go of the rope, and the cow went bounding and galloping toward her stable.

Julietta looked at him amorously, desirously, jealously. He passed by, looking at her as he looked at the woods, the sky and the fields.

She called him by his name; he was deaf to her cries, as to the bleating of the sheep, the singing of the birds and the barking of the dog.

"Arthur," she said to him, desperately. "Arthur, oh Arthur, listen!"

And she ran after him, and clung to his garments, and stammered, sobbing; her heart was beating violently, she was weeping with amour and rage. There was so much passion in those cries, in those tears, in that breast, which was heaving noisily, in that feeble and ethereal being who was dragging her knees on the ground—all that was so distant from the cries of a woman over a broken porcelain, from the bleating of sheep, from the singing of birds, from the barking of the dog, that Arthur stopped, looked at her for a moment . . . and then continued on his way.

"Oh, Arthur, please listen for a moment! For I love you, I love you! Oh, come with me, we'll live together over the sea, far from here, or even better, die together!"

Arthur was still walking.

"Listen, Arthur! Look at me! Am I, then, so very hideous, so very ugly? You're not a man, then, since your heart is as cold as marble and as hard as stone!"

She fell to her knees at his feet, falling over on her back, as if she were about to die. She was, in fact, dying, of exhaustion and fatigue. She was writhing in despair, and wanted to tear out her hair, and then she sobbed with forced laughter, and tears that stifled her voice, her knees were lacerated and covered with blood from being dragged over the stones like that; for she loved him with a lacerating, entire, satanic amour; that amour would devour her forever; it was furious, vaulting, exalted.

It really was a love inspired by Hell, with those discordant cries, that burning for which rips the soul apart and wears away the heart: a satanic passion, utterly convulsive and compulsive, so strange that it appears bizarre, so strong that it drives you insane.

"Until tomorrow, isn't it, oh Arthur? Mercy! Mercy! And I'll give you everything afterwards, my blood, my life, my soul, eternity if I had it! You can kill me if you wish, but until tomorrow! Tomorrow, on the cliff! Oh, isn't it? In the moonlight ... it's a beautiful thing, a night of amour on the rocks, to the sound of the waves, isn't it, Arthur? Until tomorrow?"

And he nonchalantly let fall from his disdainful lips two words:

"Until tomorrow!"

VII

Until tomorrow! Oh, tomorrow! And she ran like a madwoman toward the cliff, and was never seen again in the village. She had disappeared from the land.

Satan had carried her away!

VIII

It was night, the moon was shining pure and white, and, disengaged from the clouds, its light illuminated Arthur's study, the window of which he had left open. He leaned over the iron rail and breathed in the fresh nocturnal air, with delight. He heard the same sound of light and delicate feet on the tiles of his furnace, and he turned round. It was Satan, but more hideous this time, and even paler; his flanks were emaciated, and his gaping mouth allowed the sight of teeth as green as the grass of tombs.

"Well, Satan," Arthur said to him, "is it true now that I love someone? Do you believe that I've been moved by those cries, by those tears and by those forced convulsions?"

"Truly," the demon replied, quivering on his four paws, "truly, you're very insensible. And you've left her to die?"

"Is she dead?" said Arthur, looking at him coldly.

"No, but she's waiting for you."

"She's waiting for me?"

"Yes, on the cliff. Haven't you promised her? She's been there for a long time, waiting for you."

"Well then, I'll go."

"You'll go? Well, Arthur, I only ask that final mercy of you; afterwards, you can do with me anything that you please; I'm yours."

"And what do you want me to do?"

"Do you think that I care much about your soul? You'll love her, I tell you. Arthur, did you not tell me that you'd like to have passions, a mighty and burning love, different from other amours? Well, you'll have it, that amour . . . but in my turn, you'll give me your soul, won't you?"

"I don't have one."

"You believe so, but you have one, because you're a human, since you'll love."

Satan was used to seeing so much pride and vanity that he did not believe in anything but that; woe sees nothing but vice; the starving feel nothing but hunger.

"A human? Satan! Tell me, have you seen humans who can extend themselves in the air all the way to the clouds?" He deployed his green wings. "And have you seen hair like this?" He displayed his blue hair. "Have you seen in any of them a body as white as snow, Satan, a hand as strong as this?" He pinched the other's skin forcefully between his fingernails. "And finally, are there any who dare to insult you like this? Since you desire my soul, kill me right away, crush my head in your teeth, tear me apart with your claws—try, and see whether I'm human."

Satan bounded on the floor, foaming with rage, and in convulsive leaps he went to strike his back against the ceiling.

Arthur was placid. "Satan," he said to him, "you are, indeed, strong; you're powerful; I sense that you can annihilate me with a single thrust. Try, try—oh, for mercy's sake, kill me! Yes, I have a soul; I give it to you, my soul; kill me—it's easy for you, for I'm only human."

The demon leapt at his throat with an infernal cry that departed from his entrails; he tried to seize him, but the skin slid beneath his teeth. Arthur disengaged him from his breast. Satan launched himself with a furious bound, claws extended; he fell back without being able to scratch the epidermis, which was intact and polished. He bounded, furious, reckless, a raucous bark emerging from his bloodied lips, his eyes flamboyant; he stamped his feet.

Arthur lay down on the ground, his wings extended. Satan slid over him, dragged him away, crawled over him, opened his mouth to rip him; his claws were blunted as if by tearing a rock; he drooled breathlessly, red with wrath; for the first time, he found himself vanquished.

And then the other . . . the other laughed softly, and that placid laughter was as loud and sonorous, as if alloyed with a sound of iron; the burning breath that the throat exhaled repelled Satan, like the furious vibration of an alarm bell bounding into the nave, roaring, shaking the pillars and bringing down the roof.

It was necessary to see those two utterly bizarre and utterly exceptional creatures at odds, one entirely spiritual, the other carnal and divine in his matter; it was necessary to see them struggling, the body and the soul—and that soul, that pure and ethereal spirit, crawling, impotent and feeble before the haughty arrogance of brute and stupid matter.

Those two monsters of creation found themselves in one another's presence as if to hate and battle one another; it was a furious war, to the death, a terrible war . . . which had to conclude between them, as in a human being . . . in doubt and ennui.

It was two incoherent principles that were battling face to face; the spirit fell, of exhaustion and lassitude, before the patience of the body.

And they were great and sublime, those two beings, which, in combination, would have made a God, the spirit of evil and the force of power. How terrible and mighty that struggle was, with those infernal cries, that furious laughter, with the entire ruined edifice trembling underfoot, its stones shifting as if in a dream.

Finally, when Satan had leapt and fallen back on the ground many times, breathless and fatigued, his eyes dull, his skin damp with a glacial sweat and his claws broken; when Arthur had contemplated him for a long time, exhausted by rage and anger, crawling sadly at his feet; when he had savored for a long time the gasps that were escaping from his lungs, when he had contemplated the sighs of agony that he could not hold back, and which were breaking his heart; finally, when, recovered from his cruel defeat, Satan raised his weak head toward his vanquisher, he still found that automaton gaze, cold and impassive, which seemed to be laughing in its disdain.

"And you too," Arthur said to him, "allow yourself to be beaten like a human . . . and by pride again! Do you believe now that I'm telling the truth?"

"Perhaps you're not human," said Satan, "but you have a soul."

"Well, Satan, I'll go to the cliff tomorrow."

And the next day, when the concierge made his round in the corridors, he found that the flagstones were displaced and scratched in places, as if by an iron claw. The worthy man went mad in consequence.

IX

Julietta was waiting for the Duc; she waited for him day and night, running over the rocks; she waited for him, weeping; she waited for him for four years.

For the years pass quickly in a story, in thought; they flow quickly in memory, but they are slow and lame in hope.

By day, she walked on the beach, listened to the sea and looked in all directions to see whether he might be coming; and when the sun had warmed the rocks; when, exhausted, she collapsed of fatigue, she went to sleep on the sand, and then got up in order to go pick fruits, to fetch the bread that charitable souls left in a fissure in the rocks.

By night, she walked on the cliffs, wandering thus in her long white garments, her hair in disorder, with cries of dolor; and she remained thus for entire hours on a sharp spur of rock, contemplating, in the moonlight, the breakers that came to die on the strand and dissolve in white foam between the rocks and pebbles.

Poor madwoman! people said, *so young and so beautiful! Scarcely twenty years old . . . and no more hope! Well, it's her fault too; she's mad with love, love for a prince; it's pride that has doomed her, given to her by Satan.*

Yes, completely mad, indeed, of loving Duc Arthur, mad for having been unable to stifle her amour, mad for not killing herself in despair; but she believed in God, and she did not kill herself.

It is true that she often contemplated the sea and the cliff, a hundred feet high, and then she started to smile quietly, with a grimace of the lips that frightened children; completely mad for stopping before the idea of believing in God, of respecting him, of suffering for his pleasure, of weeping for his delight.

To believe in God, Julietta, is to be happy; you believe in God and you're suffering! Oh, you are, indeed, completely mad! That is what people will tell you.

But no, despair had been succeeded by dejection, furious cries by tears; no more explosions of the voice, profound sighs, but sounds spoken very softly and retained on the lips, for fear of dying in shouting them.

Her hair was white, for woe ages; it is like time, it runs quickly, weighs heavily and strikes hard; but more than that, it requires fewer tears of despair to emaciate a human being than drops of water in a storm to hollow out a tombstone; hair goes white overnight.

Her hair was white, her garments torn, but her feet were hardened by marching on the ground, scratched by brambles and thistles; her hands were cracked by the cold and the harsh ocean air, which desiccates and burns like the Northern frosts; and she was also pale and thin, with hollow and dull eyes, still vivified by a gleam of amour, which lit an infernal spark; her mouth was open, as if contracted by an involuntary and convulsive movement of the lips; but she still had a gilded complexion, burned by the sun; she still had the strange gaze that seduces and attracts; she was still the sublime and passionate soul that Satan had chosen to tempt dormant matter, body denuded of sense, flesh devoid of lust.

When she saw a man she ran toward him, threw herself at his feet, called him Arthur, and then turned away, in despair, stating: "It's not him! He isn't coming!"

And people said: Oh, the poor madwoman, so young and so beautiful, scarcely twenty years old . . . and no more hope!

It was a beautiful night, radiant with stars, all white, all azure, as calm as the sea that was tranquil and mild, and came to beat the rocks and the cliff gently.

Julietta was there, still pensive and solitary, and then—I don't know whether or not it was a dream—Arthur appeared to her.

Arthur—but oh! still cold, still calm.

"I've been waiting for you," Julietta told him. "I've been at the rendezvous for a long time." Her voice was tremulous. "Sit down with me on this rock, my Arthur, sit down. What do you need? The moon is beautiful, the stars are shining, the sea is calm, it's beautiful here, Arthur . . . oh, sit down and let's talk."

Arthur lay down beside her.

"What do you want with me, Julietta?" he said to her. "Why are you sadder than other women? Why did you ask me to come here?"

"Why . . . ? Oh, Arthur . . . but I love you!"

"What is that?"

"What? When I look at you like this, see, with this smile." She passed her arm around his waist. "When you feel my breath, when my hair brushes your mouth, well, don't you feel there, in your breast, something beating and something breathing?"

"No, no—but you're a woman; you have a soul, yes, I understand; as for me, I have no soul." He looked at her proudly. "And what is the soul, Julietta?"

"How do I know? But I love you. Oh, amour! Amour, Arthur, see, turns your hair white, like mine."

She contemplated him, drew herself over his breast, covered him with kisses and caresses; but he still remained calm under the embraces, cold under the kisses.

It was necessary to see that woman, exhausting herself with ardor, lavishing all that she had of passion, amour, poetry, devouring and intimate fire, in order to vivify Arthur's lethargic body, which remained insensible to those burning lips, those convulsive arms, like a lizard feeling the contact of a brute. Julietta was bounding with amour, as Satan was with range and wrath.

She spent many hours on Arthur's cheeks; he gazed at the azure heavens, doubtless also thinking about sublime dreams, about amours, without thinking that he had there, before him, in his arms, a celestial reality, an exceptional amour, burning and exalted.

Julietta! He let her fall, exhausted; then she tried one last effort . . . and ran toward the highest rocks and launched herself forth with a single bound. There was a silence of a few seconds, and Arthur heard the sound of a heavy body falling into the water. And the night was beautiful, utterly calm, all azure like the sea, which was mild and tranquil, its waves coming to die softly on the beach, and then the waves rolled, and fell back leaving seashells, foam and the debris of ships on the shore.

One rolled for a long time, extended, then recoiled, and then returned; it deposited something heavy and large.

It was the cadaver of a woman.

"Well?" said Arthur, looking at Satan.

And when the latter had seen that his face was still pale and smooth, that his eyes were devoid of tears, he said: "No, no! You have no soul. I was mistaken." And, looking at him enviously, he continued: "But I shall have this one."

And he sank his clawed foot into the throat of the cadaver.

X

And several centuries passed.

The earth was dormant with a lethargic slumber, no noise at its surface, and nothing could be heard but the waters of the ocean breaking into foam on the rocks;

they were furious, rising into the air turbulently, and the shore stirred at their impact as if between a giant's hands. A fine and abundant rain obscured the dubious light of the moon; the wind was breaking the forest, and the skies buckled under their breath like a reed in the breeze from a lake.

There was something in the air like a strange sound of tears and sobs; one might have thought it the last gasp of a world.

And a voice rose up from the earth and said: "Enough, enough! I've suffered for too long and bent my back—enough! Oh, mercy! Don't create another world!"

And a soft, pure voice as melodious as the voice of the angels, descended to the earth and said: "No, no, this is for eternity; there will be no other world."

SECOND SIGHT

by Pierre Véron

I had just finished reading about the trial of the latest somnambulist hauled up before the correctional police.

As I finished, I began to think that it would, in fact, be a very precious faculty for a man to be exceptionally endowed that way, with the second sight of which one so often hears mention, but which, unfortunately, has remained thus far in the state of a fantastic hypothesis.

I had scarcely sketched that mental commentary when my door opened and I saw an unknown man come in of strange appearance. He was, feature for feature, the individual once described by Frédéric Soulié in his prologue to *Les Mémoires du diable*: the same sardonic face, the same sarcastic gaze.[1]

Also as in *Les Mémoires du diable*, my bizarre visitor sat down without even waiting until I had offered him

---

1 *Les Mémoires du diable* (1837-38) was one of the classic feuilleton melodramas, which remained popular throughout the century and beyond; it describes the adventures of an amorously-inclined young aristocrat who obtains assistance from the Devil in plumbing the mysteries of the fickle female heart.

a chair, nonchalantly picked an ardent coal out of the fireplace with his crooked finger, and, having lit his cigar, said: "Pardon me, my dear Monsieur, for that unceremonious entrance, but I never make any other kind. Just now, I was strolling in the vicinity and, my gaze having chanced to pass through the walls of the house in which you live, I caught you in the process of formulating a regret and a desire . . ."

"What does this signify?" I stammered, slightly troubled. "Do you have the pretention of making me believe that you're . . . ?"

"Astaroth, Satan, Beelzebub . . . the name doesn't matter. What ought to matter to you is that the second sight, after which you seemed to me to be sighing only a moment ago, I'm in a position to give you."

"You."

"Me."

"I'd be curious, of course . . ."

"Be careful—I warn you that it's not a very brilliant gift that I'll be making you!"

"You're joking! To be able to decipher thought through skulls, to unearth all secrets, lift all veils? If nature hadn't made us as wretched and as impotent as we are, and didn't feel obliged to give us that indispensable power, is it . . . ?"

"You want it—that's understood. I won't insist; your wish is granted."

My unknown had scarcely finished that sentence than a revolution immediately seemed to take place within me. My eyes were no longer the limited organ that I had known thus far. They traversed space; they overcame all obstacles; it seemed to me that the entire world was displayed before me like a panorama.

Carried away my enthusiasm, I cried: "But that's admirable! That's sublime! That's . . ."

My speech was interrupted by the arrival of my domestic, affable and smiling, who said: "Here are the monthly accounts, Monsieur. If Monsieur will cast an eye over them . . . I've followed his prescriptions, and I'm happy to observe that I've been able to realize a considerable saving on the expenses of my predecessor. I hope that . . ."

While he was speaking, my eyes went back and forth between the page he was showing me and his face. Beneath the figures of the account, the true figures immediately appeared to me, and I was able to convince myself that I was being robbed by a good third. At the same time, I read his thoughts like an open book:

Imbecile! I'll soften you up. I've stolen a bit less than the other for the first month, and as you have the habit of being duped, you'll take me for an honest man. Triple idiot! He thinks he's cleverer than us and is scornful of us because we don't have an education. We know enough, nevertheless, to keep you in the dark.

I didn't feel the need to decipher any more. In a thunderous tone, I said: "Here's your week's notice, and do me the pleasure of decamping immediately, crook that you are!"

※

"My God, what's the matter? Whence comes that dis-
traught expression? On what grass have you been walking this morning?"

That was my friend Paul, who came in a few minutes
after the execution that I had just carried out.

My friend Paul! The cream of friends, a Pylades!

"Can you imagine, my dear chap, that I've just sacked
that wretch Joseph?"

"Has he done you a bad turn? That doesn't astonish
me; the best are worthless. But let's talk about more
serious things. I ran into the Minister yesterday in the
Comtesse de B***'s salon. He talked about you a great
deal. He likes your paintings. As you can imagine, I
agreed with him. You'll be decorated at the next Salon.
And I can say without boasting that I'll have had something to do with that . . ."

I looked my friend Paul straight in the eyes, and while
the words pressed upon his lips, I read through his pupils: *You know my friend, that charity begins with oneself:
I had myself introduced to the Minister and used your
influence for that position I covet. As for your decoration,
I'm damned if I have any desire to get mixed up in it. You
don't deserve it as much as all that, anyway, and you can
easily wait, my lad.*

Meanwhile, he was still speaking: "No, it's unworthy!" I exclaimed, suddenly. "One doesn't lie with that
impudence."

"What do you mean?"

"That you're a scoundrel, and that I've been stupid to have the slightest confidence in you—and you'll do me the pleasure of going downstairs at the double."

"You're insolent, Monsieur, and my seconds will visit you this evening."

✳

He had scarcely gone out when the doorbell rang.

"Who's that now? Damn! That rich collector who's supposed to be buying my last two paintings. Monsieur le Baron, do come in . . ."

The Baron came in, his lorgnon in his hand.

"Delightful, those two canvases, utterly delightful— that's the kind of painting I like, No, without compliments, it's quite remarkable."

Meanwhile, the satanic second sight read:

Personally, I find it frightful, but you're fashionable, my lad, and as I only have a gallery in order to pose, I have to feature you in it. Besides, you're going up, and I can probably make a profit reselling you, taking care to hurry, for your renown won't last. You're too superficial. In ten years, your daubs will no longer be selling.

"Well, what's your latest price, my friend?" said the Baron, terminating his little speech.

"None. I don't sell to idiots of your species. I'm not a grocer to haggle over the cinnamon. I don't want people just to buy my paintings, but to appreciate them. Go to all the devils."

"You're a boor or a lunatic, Monsieur. I'll tell all my friends about this, and if you receive the scrap of a commission again, I'll eat my hat."

I was suffocating. I needed air, and also consolation.

I ran downstairs after the stupid Baron. *Let's go see her*, I thought. *The sight of her will do me good.*

"Her" was an adorable creature, an ideal young woman to whom I was engaged. We were only waiting to complete the formalities before getting married.

I went in. She welcomed me with her angelic smile.

"How nice it is of you to surprise me! I didn't hope to see you during the day."

"Dear Berthe!"

"But I was talking about you with my mother. How can one forget you?"

Abomination! The second sight read:

Maman was explaining to me just now that this marriage is an excellent affair. I understand. You displease me horribly; you're too old for me, fat, gauche and disagreeable. But we're five girls in the family. Anyway, one will have consolers later. First, let's make sure of the income . . .

"Berthe!" I exclaimed, in a voice strangled by wrath. "That's infamous! Look elsewhere for a dupe; you'll never see me again."

After having run around like a madman, I found myself, I don't know how, in my armchair by my fireside.

I was weeping hot tears.

A finger was placed on my shoulder; it was the stranger from that morning.

"I told you that your wish was insensate."

"It's you! A curse upon your deadly present! I'm all alone now. In one day I've lost my best friend, the woman I loved, and my clientele; I don't even have a domestic on whom to take out my anger. All that by the fault of that infernal second sight, which . . ."

"It was you who asked for it, my dear."

"I was nothing but an imbecile."

"I don't say any different."

"Impertinent"! You'll give me satisfaction!"

"After you've crossed swords with your friend Paul."

"That's true—I forgot about that. That's another one of the felicities I owe you. Triple brute that I was to want to undo nature. But I want to avenge myself on you, at least, and you're going . . ."

So saying, I had pounced on the fire-tongs. I brandished them, and . . .

And I awoke with a start.

All of that was no more than a frightful nightmare caused by the somnambulist's trial.

The *Gazette des Tribunaux* had fallen at my feet while I was asleep. I had not lost my fiancée or my friend. I was still the painter in fashion. My domestic, more obsequious than ever, announced that my lunch was served.

I had finally recovered that precious ignorance without which life would be impossible. And I went into the dining room singing, to the tune of *Galathée*:

"Oh, how sweet it is to see nothing!"

A FATAL LEGEND

by Pierre-Alexis Ponson du Terrail

ONE evening in the autumn of 1831 people were taking tea and chatting by the fireside in the home of the young Baronne de Damfrein.

Madame de Damfrein was a widow, twenty-one years old, still in mourning, but quite ready to marry again after two years of rigor devoted to weeping for her first husband. Moreover, her choice was already made; on quitting her lugubrious garments. Madame de Damfrein was to marry Monsieur Roger de Kérouare, a former officer in the Garde Royale.

After the Baron de Damfrein's death, the Comte de Loiseray, his father-in-law, had come to chaperone the young widow during her mourning, and since then, after the first six months having been spent in complete solitude, the Baronne had reopened her drawing-room to a few friends of her husband and her father, a small number of intelligent women and an even smaller number of young men—some of those to whom the new regime had closed all doors and who, breaking their swords or ripping up their togas, would become the original stock of that idle and brilliant youth that would call itself "gilded youth" for the next eighteen years.

Among that number was Vicomte Roger de Kérouare. Handsome, bearing a slight scar on his forehead—a glorious souvenir of his brave conduct during the days of July—young and witty, he had everything logically required to turn the head of a woman of twenty widowed of a husband who had been over fifty.

Roger was an only son, rich and beloved. The Baronne was beautiful, free and similarly adored. It was a love-match rather than a marriage of convenience.

The contract was to be signed and the marriage concluded a week after the expiration of the Baronne's mourning—and it was twenty-two and a half months since Monsieur de Damfrein had died.

In the meantime, the future spouses saw one another every day. Roger de Kérouare arrived every evening at nine o'clock, sat down beside the widow to the left of the large fireplace, and they both abandoned themselves without inhibitions to the charming conversation to which love lends a mantle while it is tempered by respect and the rigid laws of society.

At ten o'clock, Monsieur de Loiseray and the dowager Madame de Langerin, the Baronne's aunt, would conclude their game of chess; the scattered groups in the drawing-room would draw together, and soon formed a circle around Madame de Damfrein, whose private conversation they had initially respected, for the sake of discretion. Then they chatted.

Often, one of the Baronne's guests took center stage and related an anecdote—and everyone would perform in turn, with the utmost grace.

That evening, the role of storyteller fell to Roger.

"There's a rather strange tradition accredited on the banks of the Loire," he said, "which concerns my family. It claims that if a Kérouare, who is an elder or only son, fails to marry before the age of twenty-five, he will die the following year; in the former case, the fief will pass to his younger brothers; in the later, the name will become extinct."

"And on what is that tradition based?" someone asked.

"On the legend that I shall relate to you."

Roger de Kérouare leaned on the mantelpiece and began, in the midst of a religious silence, the Legend of St. Paul's Protégé.

There was once, in the era of the crusades, a chatelaine named Yseult de Kérouare.

The aforesaid chatelaine had married very young and had worn the long veils of widowhood since the age of twenty-two. The Sire de Kérouare had died five years after the wedding, leaving a sole heir placed under the influential patronage of St. Paul.

Now, in the epoch when my story begins, Paul de Kérouare was nineteen years old and his mother thirty-seven. Paul was a charming cavalier, a trifle frail and a trifle timid, with large blue eyes, curly blond hair, a peach-like down on his cheeks and a feminine waist and hands. When he rode over the plain, the great ladies of the region, hidden behind the arched windows of their manses, regretted the twenty years that they no longer had, envied the twenty years that he had not yet had, and would have dearly wished to be widows if the hourglass of their oratory had not whispered to them that the wings of time had creased their white foreheads with a few slight wrinkles.

When he wandered behind the willows of the Loire, like a melancholy guardian angel in search of the poor mortal confined to his care, and whom Satan had led astray, the genteel washerwomen in their velvet corsets, the boatwomen with their braided hair and the young peasant-women with rosy cheeks scything hemp by the bank felt their young hearts beat faster, and thought that it was a great pity that he was not a humble vassal instead of a rich lord. But alas, the noble ladies, the wash-erwomen, the boatwomen and the peasant-women were wasting their time in sighing.

A league from the Manoir de Kérouare there was an-other manor, similarly leaning its gray and mossy towers over the Loire, and, just as the former manor sheltered a blond seraphim, it had for a chatelaine a young wom-an of fifteen years, pale and brunette, with dark eyes as shiny as glow-worms, and alabaster skin compared with which the marble of the archipelago was gray and poorly veined. That young woman lived with her aged father, and had no husband as yet.

Husbands were very scarce in that epoch, for two reasons—firstly, because His Majesty the King of France, when he went to fight in the Holy Land, had taken with him the flower of his fine nobility; and secondly, because in order to marry an heiress like Marguerite de Kerven it was necessary to be a noble Comte, or at least a valiant Chevalier with an escutcheon pure of any bar of bastardy, with numerous vassals and a manse surrounded by deep ditches and thick walls.

So, while awaiting a husband, the young Comtesse de Kerven went out every day, followed by a squire, at a hack gallop, through the hills, heaths and heather, unleashing her gyrfalcons or throwing her large greyhounds a silk scarf, which they brought back faithfully after contesting in agility and speed to reach it.

As really happened in those days, and still happens in today's romances, the Sire de Kérouare, out riding, and the Comtesse de Kerven, out galloping, encountered one another one day and blushed so deeply that they bowed to one another silently, not daring to speak.

The following day, hazard, that great master, did its work so well that they met one another again in the same place; the day after, the palfrey of the one and the destrier of the other grazed the same grass beside the same path behind a hedge of flowering hawthorn—and that was repeated from the dawns to the sunsets that followed— except that it is very difficult to affirm that hazard had conserved its role in that naïve comedy.

In brief, those two young hearts, which felt attracted to one another, gradually understood that the amity of man and woman is nothing other than love; and as Paul de Kérouare was rich and noble, the young Comtesse affirmed that her father would not hesitate for a moment to give him her hand, if he cared to ask for it.

Paul, as I have said, was slightly timid, and he judged it prudent to let his mother take care of the negotiations.

He therefore went to find the chatelaine and, not without blushing and paling by turns, confessed his penchant for the Comte de Kerven's daughter.

The noble chatelaine had regretted many times that she was no longer a marriageable damsel; her beauty had resisted the insults of time, and her mourning-dress suited her marvelously. The ladies of the region even claimed that she only continued to wear it out of pure coquetry, and that the Sire de Kérouare, her husband, had a tomb in her heart as solidly enclosed as the one in which his body was sealed beneath the black marble of the mortuary chapel.

Now, although she had never thought seriously about taking a new husband, the noble lady was somewhat vain regarding her beauty, and thought that her son had grown up a little too rapidly, seeming to want to push her by the shoulders toward that antechamber of ripe age that poets, being exceedingly courteous individuals, have nicknamed second youth.

Thus, great was her amazement when the young man with the golden hair, whom it pleased her to treat as a child, came to talk to her gravely about his marriage plans. That amazement was succeeded by anger; the chatelaine could not hide it from herself that, in the eyes of the malicious crowd, her son's nineteen years mounted a rude assault on the mature glare of her beauty. What would happen, then, when she had beside her a daughter-in-law of fifteen, fresh and pink, who would not take long to populate her manor with blond and cheerful children, who would give her, with a respect full of irony, the ugly-sounding name of grandmother?

In that epoch of chivalric courtesy and religious respect for the family, a son would rather have died a thousand times than disobey his mother. Madame de Kérouare had, therefore, only to reply to her son that she refused such an alliance—but that refusal would have caused him a great deal of pain, and she was a mother in spite of her coquetry.

She therefore reflected that, sooner or later, it would be necessary to go along that road, and that her obstinacy would alienate her child's heart, without shielding her from a young and beautiful daughter-in-law.

Like the intelligent woman she was, the chatelaine went to visit the Comte de Kerven and, when she returned, told her son that he could marry Marguerite, but in a few years' time, when he had won his knight's spurs on the battlefield and proved that he was not unworthy of his blood.

The good lady was so eloquent, and spoke so well about the great deeds of the Kérouare family, and the laurels to be won under the hot sun of Palestine, that the enthused Paul replied that he was ready to do anything to obtain Marguerite, and that, in order to be worthy of her hand, he felt the courage to attack Jerusalem, its forts and redoubts, on his own.

And immediately, the young Sire de Kérouare summoned his vassals and men-at-arms, had his warhorse saddled, kissed his fiancée's hand, received his mother's blessing on bended knee, and set forth, lance held high and his heart filled with masculine ardor.

As for the chatelaine, reassured by the absence of that importunate witness to her thirty-seven years, she abandoned her mourning-dress and, six months later, married a knight of a noble and ancient family, of martial appearance but very poor. In consequence, when he came to live in the Manoir de Kérouare, he brought nothing but his armor, his ragged clothing and a huge appetite. The knight in question was twenty-seven.

※

The adventurous young man disembarked, with his men-at-arms, on Egyptian soil three months after his departure from Kérouare, and took the road to the crusaders' camp, commanded by the King of France, Louis VII.

Paul de Kérouare proved everywhere that his blood was noble and boiling; the ardent desert sun bronzed his face and made his beard grow; his slender white hands were hardened by handling a battle-ax, and in three years the blond seraphim of the banks of the Loire metamorphosed into a robust and valiant knight.

Marguerite de Kerven would have been proud of him; if the Lady de Kérouare had envisaged that tall stature, that bronzed face and that thick beard, she would have applauded herself more than ever for having sent away that living proof of her forty years.

Paul de Kérouare had been fighting for three years when the king, recalled to France by his conjugal dispute with Eléonore d'Aquitaine, who was eager to barter his fleur-de-lys-ornamented crown for that of Henry of England, reassembled his knights and faithful followers and lifted the siege of Damascus, which he had been blockading for six months, in order to re-embark and return to Europe. He left behind a rearguard, however, charged with keeping the Saracens at bay, and Paul de Kérouare was among the barons and knights who stayed behind.

The crusaders had been subjected to many setbacks; the plague had decimated them; it was even worse when the king had gone. After a year, there were scarcely three hundred left, and in a final battle that they sustained with the obstinacy of despair, fifty of them were captured by the Saracens. Paul de Kérouare was among them.

The knight was taken to Tunis and sold in the slave-market. He was bought by a rich Muslim whose residence was beside the sea, and who employed him in cultivating his gardens.

Paul spent his brief hours of rest on the shore, and raised his eyes toward the mute horizon where only enemy sails were to be seen. When he thought about his manor, his mother and his fiancée, he wept. He wept because the image of the beautiful young woman was as vivid in his heart as on the day of his departure, because he would probably never see her again, nor the roof of his forefathers, nor the chatelaine de Kérouare—everything, in brief, that made life sweet and good: family and fatherland. And every day, when he resumed his rude labor, he felt weaker and more discouraged, and that terrible homesickness, complicated by lovesickness and slavery, undermined him dully and led him toward the tomb.

Finally, one day, in stifling heat, allowing himself to fall exhausted on the burning sand, he believed that he was about to die, and, remembering his young and beautiful years, and Marguerite, who was doubtless still waiting for him, he murmured: "Oh, to see her for just one hour, I would give all of those that might perhaps remain to me, and my eternal salvation with them."

Scarcely had he uttered those fateful words when a mocking voice replied: "So be it, Master—I accept, and I shall be your good prince; I'll grant you one entire day, from sunrise to sunset."

Paul de Kérouare shuddered, and, on turning round, saw a little old man sitting on the sand and contemplating him with a mocking gaze.

"Yes, Messire," he continued, "if you want to promise me your share of paradise on the word of a gentleman, you shall see Marguerite de Kerven and your mother for a full day."

"Who are you, then?" asked the astonished knight.

"My good friend," said the old man, "God gives me the name of fallen angel, and men call me Satan, but my real name is Lucifer, although I did not obtain it by baptism."

"The Devil!" Paul murmured, terrified. "Oh, I would never sign such a pact!"

"As you please—but you're going to die in a few hours."

"To die! Without seeing her again!"

"Why not?"

The knight hesitated momentarily; for a moment, Hell appeared before him with its livid flames, its sparkling laughter, its blasphemies and the crack of the metal-tipped whips that tear the bruised flesh of the damned. After all that, however, he believed that he saw a white and diaphanous robe floating in the mist; it seemed to him that the air was impregnated with the penetrating perfume that a young woman exhales as she runs through green fields amid the flowers of spring. A vague sound brought, like a sigh, the name of Marguerite to his ears—and, holding out his hand to Satan, he said: "I accept."

"Knight's honor?"

"Of course."

"Then, Master," the Devil cried, with a sinister laugh, "be satisfied, for you belong to me for eternity."

And immediately, Lucifer took the knight in his arms; his human vestments fell away; his old man's face disappeared; his eyes blazed; his wings grew and deployed—and the accursed angel took flight and launched himself through the air, carrying his victim.

For an hour that seemed to him to be a century, Paul felt himself drawn through a whirlwind of smoke, respiring the Devil's sulfurous breath, seeing nothing and hearing nothing except the sinister laughter of his terrible guide.

Then, suddenly, he felt a violent shock, as if Satan had dropped him from a height on to a rock, as an eagle might do with a lamb held in its claws. He opened his eyes, and was very astonished to find himself on the bank of the Loire, equidistant between Kérouare and Kerven.

The sun had not yet risen; dawn was sliding its silvery rays over the horizon; the birds were waking up in the crowns of the trees, the flowers bowing their dew-laden heads in the breath of the morning breeze; a light mist, similar to a veil of gauze, was floating over the waters of the river.

It was a magnificent spring day that the damned man was about to enjoy, as one enjoys one's last gold coin. And the Devil, it is necessary to admit, had shown himself to be generous, for he could have only granted his prey a dismal, damp and frosty day, instead of a spring day full of sunlight, flowers and perfumes.

In widowhood as in liberty, one has difficulty getting used to what follows. Lady de Kérouare, when her honeymoon was over, perceived that her new husband had more than one fault not mentioned in the parchments that had been scribbled during her marriage, and among those faults, she soon placed in the first rank, and by experience, a very determined desire to be the master.

The late Sire de Kérouare had been a worthy knight, but the rumor had gone around, during his life, that in his manor he quit the halberd and the lance for the skirt and distaff. Madame de Kérouare had, therefore, always been the unique arbiter of her own will; so, when the young knight to whom she had just enchained herself for the rest of her life abandoned the lover's smile for a husband's cold gravity, the noble chatelaine bucked like a stallion on to whose virgin back a bold cavalier has just launched himself. Alas, it was too late, and the yoke had been so well gorged, so solidly applied, that she had bowed her head and dropped the conjugal scepter—the emblem of authority.

Her spouse dissipated a part of the patrimony of the Kérouares, heaped taxes and rents upon the vassals, and then left one day for a tournament, in which he was killed by the thrust of a lance.

Madame de Kérouare was free again—but this time, she judged it prudent to keep her widow's independence, and began to wish ardently for the young knight's return. During her long hours of suffering, she had called out to him so many times, and during her nights of insomnia she had so often thought that she saw him lift up the heavy curtains of her bed, like a phantom, and reproach her for his death, that the unhappy woman, returned to the sentiment of maternal love, prayed night and day in her oratory, invoked all the saints in paradise, for God to return her son to her.

In the meantime, her beauty was unalterable, and the forty-third year was about to sound for her without the slightest wrinkle tarnishing the purity of her forehead, without her eyes losing their gleam and their fascinating gaze . . .

The old Comte de Kerven was dead; she had brought Marguerite to live with her, called her daughter, and no longer feared her as a rival. Kneeling, every evening, on the stone floor of the chapel, the two women implored Heaven and begged for the young crusader's return.

Finally, one night, when her eyes were red with tears, the poor chatelaine, her hands joined in her oratory, addressed a mother's prayer to the Virgin. A great light burst forth around her, and a celestial warrior, having nothing about his body but half a cloak, appeared standing before her prie-Dieu; it was Saint Paul.

"Woman," said the saint, "God has sent me to tell you that he will allow you to see your son again, but only on one condition."

"Oh!" she cried. "Let me see him for just an hour, just one, that I might press him to my heart, that I might intoxicate myself with his gaze . . . and then take my life!"

"No," said Saint Paul, "it is what remains of your beauty that God wants in exchange—the fatal beauty that sent your son away."

"Oh, Monseigneur," murmured the mother, "whiten my hair, curb my back, hollow out my cheeks and wrinkle my hands, but return my son to me . . ."

"It shall be done as you desire," said the saint. "You shall see him again tomorrow, at sunrise."

And as he finished, the chatelaine felt an icy frisson run through her body, freeze her blood and turn her heart upside-down.

"Look," said the Apostle then, presenting her with a steel mirror, which his celestial aureole illuminated.

The chatelaine darted a glance at her image, and did not recognize herself. She had white hair, her body was doubled over, her pearly teeth no longer existed, and her face, so white and so pure before, was as shiny and yellow as old parchment.

Saint Paul opened the window, and as the saints have wings as soon as they enter paradise, he flew away, taking an eastward direction, in which he had to go, on God's orders, to seek out Paul de Kérouare and bring him to his mother.

On the way, however, not far from the manor, he saw Satan cleaving the air with his wing-beats, holding his victim in his claws . . .

That unexpected encounter knocked the Devil over, and he dropped the knight, who fell heavily to the ground—where he would have fractured his skull had the saint, his patron, not deadened his fall.

Then the Apostle, insulting Beelzebub, demanded to know what this meant, and how he had dared to carry out orders that God had given to Saint Paul.

The Devil, however, recovered from his upset, replied: "It's neither for you nor for God, Master, that I'm performing this task, but on my own account, for the young man has sold me his soul."

And Satan, sitting down on a small cloud that was floating nearby, recounted what had passed between himself and Paul de Kérouare, and what bargain he had sealed.

The saint shivered, for Satan was perfectly within his rights—but immediately, a luminous idea occurred to him.

"Satan," he said, showing him the knight, still stunned from his fall and rubbing his eyes, "would you care to make a wager?"

"Two, Master, if you like."

"Look—that knight is exactly half way between his mother's château and that of his mistress. Where will he go?"

"To his mistress, by my horns! He hasn't enough virtue to sacrifice profane love to filial love."

"Well then, abstain from advising him and I'll do the same. If he takes the road to Kerven, I won't dispute either his life or his soul with you—but if, on the contrary, he takes the path to Kérouare, you'll surrender both to me."

"Oh," Satan sniggered, "have no fear!"

"Do you accept the wager?"

"Of course, for it's won in advance."

And Hell and Paradise, represented by Satan and Saint Paul, waited, motionless on the two clouds they were sitting astride, for the poor knight to decide the bet and lose or save his soul.

The Devil sniggered with the arrogantly modest smile of triumph; Saint Paul waited anxiously . . .

But suddenly, the knight's hesitation disappeared, and, turning his back on Kerven, he headed toward Kérouare with a rapid stride.

The Apostle uttered a cry of joy.

The accursed angel bit his lips, made a frightful grimace and resumed his flight, drunk with rage and shame—but he had experienced too many setbacks since his creation to allow himself to be defeated by such a minor loss; he stopped abruptly, waited until Saint Paul had disappeared among the clouds, and then launched himself in the direction of Kérouare like lightning, entering by way of a chimney and going to hide in a panel of the woodwork, from which he could see the chatelaine on her knees in her oratory, waiting for the saint's promise to be fulfilled.

As Paul got closer to the manor, he felt his heart quiver and hammer in his breast, and at the same time, a hot sweat beaded on his brow.

At the sight of those beloved places, those flowery meadows, those green trees, those hedges populated with songbirds, and the melancholy towers forming the enclosure of his manor, a host of memories disturbed his mind, coming to remind him of his happy childhood, his dreamy adolescence and his fresh amour . . .

As he arrived at the drawbridge, the sun rose and gilded the spire of the belfry.

The poor exile crossed the threshold at a run, although he was very weary, passed through a host of varlets and soldiers, who did not recognize him in his rags, climbed the large stone staircase and ran through the corridors, shouting: "Mother! Mother!"

To that shout responded another shout, uttered by a quavering voice, and a little old woman came running as fast as her debilitated legs could carry her, her arms open and tears in her eyes.

She was no longer the beautiful chatelaine, alas . . . .

But Paul threw himself into the arms that were held out to him, tenderly kissed the snowy tresses that he had left as black as ebony, covered the wrinkled hands that gripped him with caresses, and thought that he would die of joy . . .

The mother and the son embraced one another for a long time, and then Paul cried: "And Marguerite, Mother? Where is she? Does she still love me?"

"Marguerite is here," replied the old woman, coughing. "She's waiting, my child, and I'll take you to her bedside."

"Here?" said the knight. "Oh, thank . . ."

But his face suddenly darkened; a livid pallor spread over his face. "Come quickly," he said, "for I only have one day to give both of you . . ."

"What do you mean?" exclaimed the chatelaine.

"I mean," Paul murmured, dully, "that I've sold my soul in order to hug you—you and her—to my heart one last time, and that this evening, at sunset, Satan will come to take it, for I'm damned."

"Damned?" exclaimed the poor mother, with a stifled cry, collapsing like a pine-tree uprooted by a hurricane. "Damned!"

But Paul paid no heed, and continued running through the corridors to find Marguerite—and the chatelaine, thunderstruck by that revelation, remained motionless, inert, almost mad.

It was then that Satan, who had quit his hiding-place and was standing in the shadows, showed himself to her and said: "There's a simple means of redeeming your son's soul."

The old woman recoiled in terror, but Satan went on: "If you wish, your son won't be damned."

"If I wish?" she cried. "Oh, what do I have to do to soften God's wrath?"

"This," said the fallen angel, gravely, "has nothing to do with the Eternal Father, but the Devil, which is me. Your son's soul belongs to me, and that's your fault. Give me yours and I'll return his. I'll lose by the exchange, for yours is already three-quarters mine, but I'm a good fellow and I take pity on good mothers."

A smile of joy passed over the chatelaine's wrinkled face. "Oh, I accept," she said. "Take my soul, Satan; I'll suffer less in thinking that my son is saved!"

"Is that settled?"

"Yes," said the chatelaine.

"Then sign this contract." And the Devil put a pen and parchment in front of the old woman, which exhaled a frightful odor of burning.

The poor mother signed, and Satan said to her: "Go rejoin your son; you may live until sunset. Then I'll come to look for you."

With those words, Satan bowed tranquilly, put the parchment in his pocket, and rubbed his hands, saying: "There! I haven't wasted my day, and for one soul lost, I've gained another."

The chatelaine found her son at Marguerite's feet, kissing her hands deliriously and getting drunk on a joy that he thought everlasting.

The mother keeping silent about her sublime devotion, the son almost forgetting the fatal hour, the young woman ignorant of everything, the day passed in that fashion: hands in hands, eyes looking into eyes, hearts beating with a common pulsation . . .

But at the moment when the sun, having declined rapidly, arrived at the ultimate limit of the horizon, the knight and the old woman both shivered and fixed a hectic gaze on the majestic star, ready to bury itself in a magnificent shroud of orange- and red-tinted mists . . .

And holding their breath, motionless, frozen, they followed the degradation of the light in the heavens, as if their last sigh were about to be exhaled as soon as the last ray of light died away . . .

At that moment, the Devil appeared.

"Knight," he said, "your soul no longer belongs to me, but your mother has sold hers." In a strident voice he continued: "Woman, the sun has set; you have to go with me . . ."

But as the poor woman was already tottering at the approach of the wind of death, another voice, more strident and more terrible than that of the accursed angel, was heard.

"Satan!" it shouted. "This soul does not belong to you, for that of Paul de Kérouare did not belong to you when you made that woman sign the redemption of her son at the price of her eternal damnation. The woman shall live, and not go with you!" The voice was that of Saint Paul, who had just appeared on the threshold. "Woman," he added, turning to the chatelaine, "God pardons your sin in favor of your maternal love, but in order that no other will imitate you, he condemns all of your posterity, destined to perpetuate your name, who do not marry before the age of twenty-five, to die within the following year."

The Devil fled, howling with rage, and the saint returned to take his place at the foot of Jehovah's throne.

As for Paul, he married the beautiful Marguerite de Kerven the next day, on his twenty-fifth birthday.

"And that is doubtless why I am here," the narrator concluded, "occupied in telling you this true story."

"And I hope," said Madame de Damfrein, when Roger had finished, "that the prediction of the legend has never been fulfilled?"

"To tell the truth," the young man replied, "whether by pure hazard or the will of Heaven, the tradition has been justified twice."

"Get away!" said someone, with a murmur of incredulity.

"The first time, it was at Marignan, that fabulous battle which was dubbed the Combat of Giants, and before which François I, according to chivalric memory, prepared himself by sleeping, fully armed, on the barrel of a cannon. Laurent de Kérouare, aged two months fewer than twenty-six years and still a bachelor, was killed, struck by six arquebus bullets.

"The second time, it was at the terrible affair at Fontenoy. René de Kérouare, a lieutenant in the musketeers, received a cannonball full in the chest, and was carried away dead by his terrified horse. He was twenty-five years and eight months old. Fortunately, each of them had a younger brother condemned to celibacy, and the deaths obliged them to marry in order to perpetuate the name."

"Well then," said the dowager Lady de Langevin, "how old are you, Monsieur de Kérouare?"

"Twenty-five years less two months."

"It's very fortunate," replied Monsieur de Loiseray, "that the Baronne's mourning expires in six weeks, for if your twenty-fifth year found you a bachelor and the fatal tradition were accomplished, you wouldn't even have a brother to continue the family."

"Indeed," said Roger. "I'm an only son." And he darted a tender and respectful glance at the widow.

"Bah!" said various people. "Fairy tales, all that!"

"You can make fun of me if you wish," said Madame de Damfrein, laughing, "but I believe in traditions."

The most incredulous contented themselves with smiling, and everyone retired.

Madame de Danmfrein went to her room anxious, did not sleep at all that night, and was agitated by a thousand crazy fears.

The next morning, at eight o'clock, her chambermaid came in silently, and, finding her awake, told her that Monsieur de Kérouare was asking to see her.

"At this hour" cried the Baronne. "What's wrong? My God, what's wrong?"

She put on a dressing-gown, put slippers on her feet, put a mantlet over her shoulders, and said: "Show Monsieur de Kérouare into my boudoir: I'll be in shortly."

Roger de Kérouare was in traveling costume, with a riding-crop in his hand and an anxious frown on his face.

"My God!" cried Madame de Damnfrein, when she came in. "What's the matter, Roger, and where are you going?"

"What's the matter?" he said, kissing her hand. "The anxiety of mystery. Where am I going? To Kérouare."

"Is your father ... ?"

"Ill? No; he's very well."

"Your aunt ... ?"

"In perfect health."

"What is it, then? Explain."

"Impossible—I know absolutely nothing myself. Yesterday, when I got home, I found Antoine, my father's old domestic, who gave me this note. Read it."

The Baronne took it, and read:

My son,
Put everything aside, interrupt all your plans, mount a fast horse and come here.
Comte de Kérouare.

"But your domestic must have told you . . ." said the Baronne.

"Antoine knows absolutely nothing. My father has been receiving many letters for several days; he is visiting his neighbors urgently, and seems increasingly agitated, but has not said a word."

"My God!" the widow murmured.

"Dear soul," Roger replied, "have no fear. Whatever my father's wishes are, my life is yours, and for always."

"Your life, Roger? Look, in two months, you'll be twenty-five, and if we're not married, then . . ."

"Good," said the young man. "Do you believe my legend?"

"Well, yes, I believe it. I had a presentiment of everything that is happening, for I didn't sleep last night."

"Silly!" said Roger. "In any case, it only takes two days to go to Kérouare, as many to come back, and I have plenty of time. My sharpest pain is that separation."

"Write to me when you arrive."

"Before I take my boots off—don't worry."

The future spouses made their tender adieux, full of regrets and hopes. Then Roger mounted up, and took the road to Angers, at a gallop.

Roger de Kérouare to Madame la Baronne de Damfrein Kéramoure . . . . 1831.

Dear Angel,

I've arrived. I've found Kérouare just as I left it in June of last year, except that the trees in the park, deprived of their leaves, are creaking lugubriously under the effort of the autumn wind; the swallows have gone, the meadows are burned by frost, and the banks of the Loire are heart-breakingly sad.

I found my father leaning, as is his custom, against the mantelpiece of the large fireplace in the drawing-room—formerly the armory. My aunt, Mademoiselle de Kérouare, was huddled in her armchair beside the fire, her dog Azor at her feet and her triple-layered lace bonnet on her head. She was rereading, for at least the third time, the late Crébillon fils' *Le Sopha*. My father was silent and severe, with his eagle's nose and his short-cropped white hair. He offered me his hand, silently, indicated an armchair to me, and sent away the domestics who had introduced me, in accordance with the old French custom, pronouncing my title and my name.

In the meantime, I couldn't help examining the family portraits that are hanging on the walls of the drawing-room, and perhaps I never felt as much respect for those grave and mute individuals—a historical pageant recalling in their costumes all the reigns, from the halberds and helmets of the crusaders to the gold-embroidered red uniforms of the king's musketeers.

When the three of us were alone, my father sat down and said: "Roger, you're brave, I know."

"That's a very feeble merit when one's name is Kérouare," I said.

"Since the July catastrophe returned you to civilian status a year ago, have you changed your principles?"

"Oh, Father, I didn't expect such an insult or suspicion!"

"That's good," he said. "In that case, the time has come to take up your sword again."

"What do you mean, Father?"

"That *Madame*[1] has been in the Vendée for three days, that I am one of the leaders of the uprising that will take place in the West, and that we're leaving this evening."

"Very well," I replied. "I'm ready."

Then the Comte de Kérouare asked me for your news, talked to me about our impending marriage, and when, in spite of myself, I recalled the popular legend that has weighed upon our family for five centuries, he said: "Bah! You have two months ahead of you, and we'll only need one to open the gates of Paris to His Majesty."

It's now two o'clock; we shall mount up at nightfall, and reach the Vendée at the gallop.

Adieu, dear angel—or, rather, *au revoir*. I'll write to you when I can. It's a perilous enterprise on which we're about to gamble our heads and the salvation of our

---

1 The reference is to the Duchesse de Berry, who provoked the rising in the Vendée that was intended to win back the French throne for the Bourbons; the deposed Charles X had taken refuge in Scotland, but was said to have agreed to surrender his right to the throne he had abdicated to his young grandson, the Duc de Bordeaux, whom the legitimists called "Henri V." The Duchesse de Berry was his mother, who would have ruled as regent had the insurrection been successful, but it was soon put down.

cause, but when has love in one's heart and one takes up the sword for one's king, death retreats and victory takes its place.

> I am covering this letter with kisses.
>
> Roger.

✳

Roger de Kérouare to Madame la Baronne de Damfrein
...... Vendée, November 1831.

It is exhausted by fatigue, with my hand on my rifle, the stormy sky for a ceiling, a forest for wallpaper and a haversack for a writing-desk that I am writing to you, dear angel. It's painful to say, but in our first encounter, we have been smashed and overwhelmed by force of numbers. We're battling like lions; my father and I are safe and sound. I'm putting my entire soul into your heart, and I'm pronouncing your name in a whisper, telling myself that perhaps I shall see you soon.

> Adieu,
>
> Roger.

✳

A month had gone by since the receipt of that letter, and Roger had reached his twenty-fifth year.

Madame de Damfrein, after having put away her widow's weeds and awaiting her fiancé, began to yield to crazy terrors. Apart from the continual danger that he was in, she thought incessantly about that fatal legend.

Every day she devoured the issue of the *Quotidienne* that gave the number of the dead and their names. Roger's was nowhere to be found; then she began to breathe again. In the evening, her terrors returned, until the following day, when she read an almost-identical line: "After prodigies of valor, Monsieur le Comte de Kérouare and his son have withdrawn safe and sound."

Finally, one evening, someone announced:

"Monsieur de Kérouare."

The Baronne uttered a cry of joy, and turned to the door.

Instead of Roger, however, she saw an old man, grave and austere, dressed in black, who came to her and silently kissed her hand, while he held out a handkerchief spattered with blood, and a gold ring encasing a fine pearl.

At the sight of that ring—the one she had given to Roger—the poor woman uttered a cry of despair, and fell in a faint on to the parquet.

When she came round, the Comte was at her bedside.

"Madame," he said, "Roger died a brave gentleman, and if the sight of a greater dolor can soften another, I say to you: Look at this old man; he has seen his king depart into exile, his son fall at his right-hand side, and he will descend alone into the tomb of the Kérouares, which will close forever on them and on him, for he has no scion . . ."

And the old gentleman, finally broken by grief, hid his head in his hands and wept.

The legend had completed its work.

The Comte died within the year—and Madame de Damfrein, after having wept for Roger for a time, ended up marrying again.

It is only a father's dolor that is mortal.

BURNED TEARS

by Catulle Mendès

THAT poets, even the most mediocre, are provided, in regard to their estate—which is to say, Dreams, Amour and Pity for the poor—with a very particular understanding, and also with a science refused to popes, emperor, kings rabbis, doctors and other omnipotent or omniscient individuals, is a truth that, if contested, would emerge from the contest even more evident; and, if they can be refused the art of politics or war, theologies or scientific inventions—in my opinion, they are refused wrongly, for the mere possibility of a beautiful sonnet or pleasing rondeau implies, in effect, the knowledge of power of Everything—it cannot be denied that, by nature, poets excel in the divination of sublime chimeras, in the adoration of splendid dreams and in the tears that console human dolors.

Engineers pretend to be unaware that the means of locomotion commonly known as the railway was imagined by the Persian poet Firdausi, as one can be convinced by reading in the Book of Kings the description of the steam elephants that King Iskander sent forth against the army of King Phur, but they are obliged to recognize that the good news of the hope of the Beautiful and of Mercy were brought to humans by those who make verses; with the consequence that you will not experience any astonishment on learning from me (I obtained the certainty of it from a legend engraved on a palm leaf by a beggar-poet of the time of Saint Mary of Egypt[1]) that, for many centuries, the infernal punishments with which devout souls are so justly preoccupied, have been abolished in fact, if not in law.

There is no more Gehenna; there are no more eternal tortures; and, to tell the truth, paradise is accorded to the worst sinners on earth as easily as to simple girls who died in innocence before even putting on the short skirt that is the commencement of damnable perversity.

That is a fine encouragement to persons inclined to the seven deadly sins, notably that of lust, which is the most frequent, being the sweetest to commit and the most similar to Good because of the beauty of the arms and breasts that invite you to it. In any case, it is as I say; and, precisely by virtue of an excess of antithesis explained by the infinity of mercy, it is to Our Lady Mary, the paragon of celestial virtues, that we owe the sure hope of not being chastised for our crimes on earth. But it is necessary to tell the tale of that fortunate change; and I shall do so by translating for you, in French prose, the poem invented by the beggar-poet at the very moment when the repentant Egyptian was traversing the Nile without her bare feet, which the crocodiles adored, sinking beneath the surface.

---

1 i.e. the fourth century A.D.

※

It is averred in all times and confirmed by the most authentic sacred texts that, as at the gates of our cities, there is a tollbooth at the gates of Heaven.

At the beginning of time, angelic tax-collectors with partially deployed wings asked souls arrived from earth after corporeal death: "Have you anything to declare?" and, in accordance with what they declared or did not declare, they were permitted or refused entry. But there were abuses. Sinful spirits dissimulated their sins, just as it happens every day that clever smugglers do not admit to the bottles of alcohol concealed under their clothing or, in their vehicles, under vegetables being transported to market. And fraud populated paradise with scarcely commendable souls, entirely appropriate to adulterate the purity of the recent Elect and the ancient Elect.

As pure as a ring-dove but as wily as a monkey, the Holy Spirit found a means to ward off such a great inconvenience. There were balances henceforth at the door to the Blissful Abode, which Saint Peter held in the air and in which, the sins on one pan and the virtues on the other, the merits and demerits of the soul that wanted to enter into Eternal Joy were weighed. Whichever pan, being heavier, descended, decided the fate of the candidates. They rose up or were engulfed, in accordance with the proof, toward Heaven or Hell.

That was well imagined! But it was not long before it was perceived in Heaven that the Devil, desirous of increasing the population of his empire, and who, as was only just, had obtained permission to witness the proof of the Balance, had found a means of taking possession of a large number of souls that were not his due. He quibbled over the equality of the balance-pans, and affirmed that dead humanity was being saved at false weight; to hear him, the sole venial sin of a nun who had sighed while watching a young curate pass by should have outweighed a heap of innocences, prayers, fasts and penitences accumulated on the other pan. In addition, he cheated. Slyly, half turned away, seemingly thinking about something else, he hooked the pan with the tip of a claw in the direction of Hell.

Saint Peter, a good fellow, whose sight was slightly troubled by the serenity disturbed by the third crow of the cock, did not see any of these underhand practices, and the tenebrous empire filed up immeasurably to the detriment of the celestial Eden.

Oh, how chagrined Our Lady Mary was by that! For she is the Mother of elect souls, and the more children she has the more content she is. As God the Father could refuse her nothing—he certainly owed her that compensation—she easily obtained permission from him to witness the proof of the Balance, on the sole condition that she would be completely hidden under a veil: a veil of cloud and a veil of stars; a veil which, by virtue of dazzling, did not allow either her virginal visage or the divinely material bosom to be seen—for it is inappropriate for Evil to contemplate Beauty, and one is no less jealous for being God.

At first, matters regarding the two pans passed rather equitably; Lucifer would not have dared to stoop to sly pettifogging before the radiant simplicity of Mary, and he even renounced subterfuge, not risking the trickery of the claw that made the balance tilt, because of the eyes behind the veils, which he sensed to be so pure and so perspicacious—and equity presided over Judgment for a long time.

But how troubled the saintly Virgin Mary was by so many souls whose sins, by weight, prevailed over the weight of their virtues! She had so much compassion that it cost her to have justice. Alas, Hell lasts so long, and so, in spite of the hope of an end, does Purgatory! Was it truly necessary that, for a little too much Anger or Envy, Sloth or Pride, so many souls should descend into the formidable tortures of punishment? And she, the Virgin of virgins, would even have liked to spare the culpable souls issued from libertine bodies those tortures. Heaven is amour too! And she did not know what sin there could be in the kiss, not having known the pleasure of it.

Always thickly concealed by celestial veils, and so beautiful beneath them, clemency led her to attempt to enter into an accommodation with the Devil. She tried to persuade him that it was not just to be so just, and that, in sum, no great wrong would be done if a few souls that ought to have been his went to her, a little unduly. Above all, being so pure, she felt sad because of chastised courtesans, and she had for the unknown mud the condescension of snow.

But the Devil persisted in his strict rights, and dragged souls that were too heavy on the evil pan to Hell, feet first.

Then, it came about that, Lucifer no longer cheating, it was Our Lady Mary who cheated in her turn.

Oh, how much cunning she put into it, without any appearance of it! Standing alongside the pan of merits, when all hope that it might prevail was lost, she pretended, beneath her long veils, to be almost disinterested, turning away as if indifferently—for this time, needless to say, the Devil was in the right—but, with the adroit abandonment of the flap of her sleeve, she weighed the pan whose inclination would have decided the election of a soul; or, with the nail or her little finger, she tried to hook on to and bring down the excessively light elevation of Christian merits.

Lucifer is not one of those who can be mocked; in addition, he had noticed that, not content with the weight of the flap of her sleeve or the heavy subtlety of her little finger, Madame God—as the evil tongues of Hell, where there are journalists, call Mary—risked the impudence of her clemency to the extent of dropping into the pan of salvation, sometimes a ring, one of those that the Eternal had put on her fingers, and sometimes one of the diamonds of the pendant earrings that she had in the pink lobes of her ears, or, one after another, the pearl-stars of the Milky Way, which she had around her neck under her veils.

And the Devil was annoyed.

Accustomed to talking to the Lord since the prologue in Heaven of Goethe's *Faust*, he demanded—and the Almighty, who is also Absolute Justice, had to comply— that Our Lady Mary should only witness the operations of the paradisal tollbooth deprived of luminous gems capable of weighing down one or other pan of the balance.

The ever-compassionate mother of the tender Jesus no longer had any jewels under her veils. Now what would she do? How could she cheat? By means of what ruse could she weigh down the decisive pan of Salvation?

And, because of a poor girl who, for having loved too much down here, was about to suffer eternally, she wept. She wept tears: so many tears that they weighed down the pan and saved the amorous woman.

And from that moment on, she only any longer employed, in order to save souls from Hell, the single stratagem, so sincere, of pity.

At every proof, in the pan that threatened to be insufficiently heavy, her love for the disinherited, the abandoned and the culpable wept.

Now, the Devil had nothing to say. He did not have the right, in sum, to prevent the Virgin from weeping.

But who knows whether, finally tortured by his eternal hatred, he too did not come to know pity for those he would torture? Either by virtue of natural clemency, the memory of former divinity, or supreme subterfuge—I incline to the last hypothesis—he began shedding abundant, and heavier tears—oh, how much heavier!—in the pan that inclined toward Hell.

In response to trickery—trickery and a half!—Evil prevailed, by means of tears, or the simulation of tears.

And all souls fell toward Gehenna, and there was no longer, even for repentant souls, the joy of Heaven.

Our Lady Mary foresaw her defeat, and a Paradise without Elect, and the supplication of joined hands hammering at the closed doors of Justice. And Mary looked at Lucifer. He was still handsome, for having been an angel; it was impossible that there did not subsist, in his vanquished pride, from his ancient felicity, a little tenderness.

Sublimized by the habitude of Heaven, a memory of the triumph of her charms awoke in her pure soul of a young girl once regarded complaisantly by young men when she brought the midday meal to the good black-smith who smiled at his beautiful wife, and she thought that one could tempt the Devil, since the Devil had tempted God . . .

While the clever damnatory tears fell on the pan of Hell, she suddenly took off all her veils of clouds and stars, and, with her face and breasts naked, she looked at Lucifer. He looked at her too, forgetting to be frightful, radiant for having been dazzled.

Softly, she continued weeping into the divine pan of the Balance; but he, looking at her, contemplating her, possessing her with his eyes, in which the ardent aurora of ancient mornings revived, was no longer able to weep, his tears burned by the radiant apparition of virginal Glory . . .

. . . And for a long time they have been standing thus, facing one another; and that is why all souls are now saved.

THE CLOCK

by Jean Richepin

WITH a grave and slightly cracked voice, melancholy in its timbre in the calm evening air that it rent with an abrupt sob, the first stroke of seven rang out from the bell-tower of the Hôtel de Ville.

Like soldiers on parade, whose automatic gesture is triggered by a command, all the pedestrians in the Mall came to a halt, reached for their fob-pockets, took out their watches, checked the time on the dials of the watches, put them back into their fob-pockets, shaking their heads sadly, and raised their arms to the heavens.

Then, with a voice as melancholy in its timbre as that of the bell-tower, almost with sobs like the ones continuing to rend the calm evening air, they said to one another, in tearful groups:

"I make it five to seven myself."

"Me, five past seven."

"Me, two minutes past seven."

"Me, three minutes to seven."

"Me, one minute to."

"Me, half a minute past."

But none—absolutely none—showed exactly seven.

And as an old man appeared in the Mall at that moment, heading toward the Église des Génovéfains,[1] all gazes bombarded that old man with reproaches, which were no less indignant for being silent, some even going so far as to manifest not merely indignation but scorn, and some, even a veritable horror.

The old man, however, did not present, either in his gait or in his physiognomy, anything seemingly capable of inspiring such a violent, undisguised and unanimously vengeful antipathy.

He was dressed in the most decent fashion, which denoted the most respectable of bourgeois individuals. His shoes were coarse, but well-polished. His trousers, a little too short, were not frayed. His jacket, a little too long, only gave a little more majesty to his tall stature. Besides which, age had not curved that stature, which the old man held upright with the special pride that is the prerogative of a clear conscience.

His clean-shaven face, pale beneath long white hair, was not content, as they say, to respire honesty; it positively transpired it—and the two most luminous droplets of that venerable transpiration were the old man's eyes: two eyes of pure diamond, In which shone, simultaneously, a mystical exaltation, a child-like candor, a patriarchal serenity and a heroic valor.

What secret reasons, then, could have led all those pedestrians in the Mall—and, by their mute intermedi-

---

1 Genovefa is the Latin form of the French Geneviève, the name of a legendary saint widely revered for having saved Paris from Attila's Huns by fervent prayer, who became the guiding light of an order of canons and nuns that spread throughout France in the 17th century.

ary, the entire town—to manifest toward the old man so much indignation, and so much scorn, not to say horror.

That is what you will begin to understand, or at least to suspect, when you know that the old man was the only clockmaker in the little town, that all the church clocks, pendulum clocks and pocket watches in the town were regulated by him, that they had always kept time admirably for more than thirty years, and that he was presently neglecting them.

But why was he neglecting them at present? Through what breach had his disrupted professional honorability fled? How had that pure gold been transmuted into vulgar lead? Ah, that's a long story! Listen, instead, to the reflections of the people.

"Look, he's going to spend the night at the Église des Génovéfains again."

"He'll be there until tomorrow morning with his folly."

"Then, naturally, during the day, he can't do any more."

"And he resets watches any old how."

"And he goes to sleep over the pendulum clocks, instead of watching over them as before."

"He doesn't even bother with the Hôtel de Ville clock any more."

"He doesn't care about anything but the old clock over there."

"And I ask you, what's the point? He's mad—completely mad."

"Obviously, since the cleverest haven't been able to make head nor tail of it."

"He'll come off worse than that, mark my words."

"The clientele comes first, doesn't it? Like me . . ."

"Me too, of course! Just let another clockmaker set up in business here, and we'll see, once and for all."

"One's coming from Saint-Jean, I've been told."

"So much the worse for Père Bringard. He'll die of starvation."

"Unless he dies of old age before then . . ."

"That might be the best thing for him. There's danger over there."

"Oh, not only danger from machines, you know!"

"Yes, yes, I know—even more so from legends."

"Exactly. Is it true or isn't it? Still, our forefathers were no more stupid than we are, eh? Well, they believed, and firmly, that one couldn't touch it without it bringing you bad luck."

"Which doesn't prevent the old madman from running off yet again, to spend all night flirting with his old vagabond witch of a clock."

For it is, in fact, a matter of a clock. At the Église des Génovéfains there is an ancient clock, one of those fabricated in the Middle Ages by patient workmen who consecrated their entire lives to it, multiplying its cogwheels, its pulleys, its weights and its counterweights in order that, at the hours of the Angelus, one would hear it sing interminable and cheerful carillons, while from its face, opening like a tabernacle, the Holy Virgin would emerge, to whom the Angel Gabriel bowed, and before whom filed in slow procession the holy apostles, six for the morning Angelus and six for the evening Angelus, and all twelve for the midday Angelus.

Now, for many years, if not forever, the ancient clock of the Église des Génovéfains had been broken down—and there were, indeed, legends about that: like the one asserting that the master clockmaker who had constructed it had only completed the task with the aid of the Devil; and the one claiming that, after a certain number of revolutions, the Devil had stopped the clock; and the one declaring that the secret of it had been lost forever, and that misfortune befell anyone who tried to recover that secret—and a whole string of stories embroidered on that subject by the popular imagination.

Today, of course, hardly anyone believed any longer in those legends and stories. A few people still talked about them, but only to laugh at them. But Père Bringard, personally, did not laugh at them. And, by dint of thinking about them, after thirty years of long meditation, he had ended up believing in them.

In particular he believed this: that the soul of the master clockmaker of old had been a captive of the Devil since the day the clock stopped working, and that the poor soul in question would be liberated when the clock worked again. And, mostly thanks to that charitable hope, and also a little because of his pride as a clockmaker, he had harnessed himself to the task of repairing the clock, putting all his patient ingenuity into the task, and all his faith.

To the very few friends who remained to him, and who took pity on his madness, and tried to cure him of it, he replied confidently: "I'll get there. I've already done this and that. One more exact weight to find, of a particular metal, and the clock will work, you'll see."

Meanwhile, he spent all his time and his nights on it, and neglected all the clocks and watches in the town, and became an object of indignation, of scorn, and even of horror—but he had not been cured, and had redoubled his efforts toward his chimera, wanting to attain it before dying, and thinking every day that he was a little closer to the point of attaining it, and passing through the hostile groups, repeating like a chorus: "Tonight I'll surely be finished. It will be tomorrow, at midday. Tomorrow, at midday, the clock will work. Tomorrow, at midday. Tomorrow, at midday."

But the days went by without the clock working— and now, urchins followed Père Bringard through the streets, yapping: "Hoo! Hoo! Have you made it work, the Delusion? Tomorrow, at midday. Tomorrow, at midday."

And yet, one fine day, at midday, from the belfry of the Génovéfiens, the carillon rang out, *ding ding dong*, singing its joyful song, while from the face of the clock, opening like a tabernacle, the Holy Virgin emerged, to whom the Angel Gabriel bowed, and before whom filed in slow procession the twelve apostles.

A miracle! A miracle!

People ran from all over town. They searched for Père Bringard to give him an ovation. They cried that he was the glory of the region. They waxed ecstatic before the resuscitated clock. Miscreants were weeping with joy.

But Père Bringard could no longer hear anything, or see anything. From one of the chains of the clock, in the guise of a weight—liberating the soul of the master clockmaker of old by finally making his beloved work— the old man had hanged himself.

ANOTHER SOUL SOLD TO THE DEVIL

by Léon Gozlan

I

"IT'S strange! It's distressing! It's enough to make one throw oneself in the Seine, or to poison oneself with the rest of the Chinese vermilion in the bottom of that bladder," the young artist Mandanne said to himself, miserable, haggard, crazed and desperate, as he gazed with convulsions of rage at a painting set in front of him. "Me, refused by the jury! Refused! Yes, refused, in the most odious fashion possible."

He plunged his clenched fists into his pockets, stamping on the parquet, to the point of making his plaster casts and skeletons tremble in every corner of the studio. "What, then, does one have to do?" he murmured. "I consulted my friends while I was working on my painting; I listened to all their criticisms, welcomed all their advice, and retouched my subject bit by bit, in a thousand different places—everywhere, in sum. The composition, design and colors have been redone relentlessly—and after all that trouble, care, late nights and time, a refusal! Tomorrow, the newspapers will publish my defeat and my shame—the newspapers, those consolers who enlarge wounds with the intention of healing them. Tomorrow, the stepfather of the woman I was to marry will send me away, and my landlord will tell me to get out of his house, under the pretext of repair and decoration; tomorrow, my porter will say to me: 'What do you expect?' Tomorrow . . . but tomorrow, I shall be dead."

Mandanne fell silent momentarily in order to concentrate his dolor on his refused painting, a painting forty feet in circumference, encased in a magnificent frame, representing the most poetically beautiful mythological theme: *Time Discovering Truth.*

"Yes," he went on, with a new bitterness, "the time to discover, one day soon, the truth of my merit, my talent, the charm of my work; but I shall no longer be alive, I shall be with all the great persecuted artists, with . . ." At this point Mandanne recited a long litany of the martyrs of art, and was not consoled.

"Let's be done with it," he added, going to the far end of the studio to look for one of those poor painter's inkwells in which there is everything but ink. He succeeded nevertheless in tracing a few lines on a piece of paper on which there was the beginning of a caricature: *I die innocent, and after my death I want my painting of* Time Discovering Truth *to be given to Champigneulles, my birthplace.*

Then he picked up his hat in order to go and drown himself opposite the Louvre, a few meters from the monument where he had been refused. He was very fond of the place.

"One more look at my work," he said to himself—and he paused, tears in his eyes, a few paces away from the painting proscribed by the warrant of the members of the Institut. The sun, as it set, cut diagonally through the cage of his studio and illuminated the only two figures in his vast canvas. The effect of the light, as usual, lent considerable value to the painter's subject—a charm that it does not always have in reality. The setting sun is a flatterer.

The veil that Time, suspended in mid-air, was lifting seemed delightfully light, and Truth was rendered with a great seduction of color. To Mandanne, everything seemed perfect, incomparable and sublime: the head of Time, his gray beard, his knock-kneed legs, fading backwards into the clouds, and the face of Truth, her colors, her hands and her expression. Raphael had passed that way, but a Raphael enriched by three centuries of progress, humanitarian ideas and a thousand other improvements.

Mandanne choked with despair as he drowned himself thus in his superiority, before going to drown himself in the Seine opposite the Louvre.

"There would be reason enough to give oneself to the devil a thousand times over," he exclaimed, as he opened the door of his studio, "if the devil existed—but he no longer exists . . ."

At this point, Mandanne was about to proffer a horrible blasphemy, and that is doubtless what brought forth, violently, the individual with whom he found himself face to face as he extended his leg toward the first step of the staircase.

"I beg your pardon," said a man dressed in a black velvet overcoat and wearing furry gloves, "but I exist."

"Are you . . . ?"

"I'm him."

"That's implausible," said Mandanne.

"I don't deny it. But what is plausible? Is it plausible that one would drown oneself for a painting?"

"Do you think it's bad too?"

"I don't say that; I don't say anything. You wanted me; I've come. I can only prove to you that I exist by giving you evidence of my power. Speak!"

"Make all the members of the jury die of apoplexy right away, and I'll believe you."

"What good would that do you?"

"None, in fact; my painting would still have been refused."

"Ask me for a useful impossibility, and you'll see."

"All right! That my painting of *Time Discovering Truth* should be transformed instantly, that its subject should be changed, and that, having been taken before the jury, it has been accepted."

"That's child's play. Your soul's worth more."

"You want me to sell my soul, then?"

"Since you don't believe in me, what risk is there in signing the pact?"

"It's just that you're unsettling me . . ."

"Hurry up, young man; I have a deal to make with a minister before ten o'clock this evening, and another with a young woman before midnight. My minutes are precious."

Mandanne went pale.

"But if I accept," he stammered, "will I at least have a good place at the Salon?"

"The best."

"You assure me?"

"You'll have the king's corner, when he's painted with the Garde Nationale . . ."

"You're tempting me."

"That's my trade—and not only will you obtain the most favorable place in the gallery of the Salon, but you'll have eulogies in all the newspapers, you'll be awarded the croix d'honneur, you'll have commissions, you'll give audiences to the director of the Beaux-Arts—in sum, you'll have everything that you desire."

"It's agreed, then," said Mandanne, who had become accustomed to the devil, as one becomes accustomed to the Garde Nationale, "that our pact will last throughout my life, that you won't have the right to limit it."

"It's agreed—but as soon as your final hour sounds, I'll be there to take your soul."

"But what will you do with it?"

"Ah—that's my secret!"

"Bah!" said Mandanne, after a few moments' hesitation. "I might as well be burned for one thing as another!" He extended his hand to the devil, who had the prudence to withdraw his own, and cried: "I accept!"

"You swear to be mine?" the tempter said to him.

"I swear."

"Raise your eyes," the devil said to him then, "and look."

Mandanne looked.

He was at the Salon, in the midst of three or four thousand people, who, at close range and from afar—from every distance—had their eyes fixed upon a magnificent portrait in oils representing the wife of a famous notary. The portrait was signed "Mandanne."

II

And this is what people around him were saying:

"Has a better resemblance ever been seen? What fire! What originality! What vigor! What relief! It's as beautiful as the portrait of François I by Titian, or that of the old pensioner by Van Dyck."

"Leave off!" murmured young people coiffed in red caps. "Titian and Van Dyck aren't worthy to wipe Mandanne's brushes."

Mandanne blushed; justice was being rendered to him.

"And when one thinks," they added, "that an artist like him isn't decorated, while bushels of crosses and ells of ribbon are thrown at chapel daubers whose only merit is knowing how to wait every day for twenty years in the corridors of the ministry for the director of the Beaux-Arts to pass by, in order to kiss his boots."

The opinion of serious people was, extraordinarily, in perfect accord with that of those young hotheads—not that they disparaged Van Dyck and Titian to raise up Mandanne, but they all agreed that nothing as gripping had been seen in painting since those old masters.

"Don't you think, though," Mandanne hazarded to say, with a timidity that still reflected the modesty of his former obscurity, "that the forehead is a little too much in the light?"

"It's your eyes that aren't sufficiently in it," a red cap immediately replied to him.

"Let's help Monsieur to see a little better," added another cap, lifting Mandanne three feet off the floor.

"To the lantern!" shouted a third. "There's no lack of light there!"

So, for having risked a very feeble criticism of himself, Mandanne was about to pass through one of the Louvre's large windows, and perhaps fall into the same river in which he had wanted to drown himself a few hours before.

The danger was not, however, without charm for him; he would gladly have thanked his murderers if they had permitted him to speak, but they were strangling him; all that he could do, in that situation, was smile at them. He would doubtless have died asphyxiated if an energetic flood coming from the door had not caused a powerful diversion among the group of frantic admirers in the midst of whom the glorious and unfortunate Mandanne was choking.

That undulation brought admirers of a more elevated sphere before Mandanne's painting. Members of the four academies could be distinguished, officers of the king's household and that of the princes, and, in their midst, the Minister of the Interior—who, after having congratulated, embraced and introduced Mandanne to the ambassadors associated with that ovation, awarded him with his own hand the Civil and Military Order of the Légion d'honneur.

One can easily imagine the astonishment of the two or three hundred pupils seeing the great artist Madanne honored in that fashion, in the person of the man of whom they had almost made a victim. A singularity worthy of note is that none of them, suddenly changing his opinion of the merits of the recompensed painter, said: "Another donkey decorated while so many illustrious artists, such as Trillebardou, Chantefouille and the great Crapoussin, are neglected!" Madanne was deemed pure, although fortunate. He was carried around the gallery three times, and applauded like a bad tragedy.

The happiness of his first day of glory was not to stop there. On returning home, he found two letters, one large and square, the other oblong and perfumed. He opened the latter first, for he was not yet thirty, and read:

Monsieur,

Renown has borne your name into the depths of my boudoir; if you do not think me unworthy of your brushes, come to my home, the Hôtel d'Armainville in the Rue de la Ferme, before noon tomorrow. You will find a model as docile—I dare not say beautiful—as you desire.

Your admirer,
Comtesse Burgos.

"I'll begin with the Comtesse," Mandanne murmured. "Where shall I end up? Let's see what the second letter contains."

Again, he read.

Monsieur,

I am instructed to tell you that Monsieur le Ministre de l'intérieur grants you a gratification of 20,000 francs from the funds of the Beaux-Arts. You may present your-self to the treasury to collect your mandate.

"It appears," said Mandanne, whose wit had not yet been eroded by prosperity, "that my soul is of the finest quality."

Those who might have been tempted to set the perfectly true, though seemingly fantastic, story of Mandanne in the present era will immediately have realized their error on seeing a Minister of the Interior recognize, reward and decorate merit. No allusion to the present time is possible; the remuneratory fact is sufficient proof of that.

Mandanne placed the letter from the Ministry of the Interior under his head and the note from Comtesse Burgos over his heart, and did not get a wink of sleep.

No one will be astonished to hear that he expected at any moment to see the devil come into his room, in order to obtain an account of the day's complete suc-cess, but the devil did not appear. As a gallant man, a man who knows how to behave, he has no need of grat-itude—and besides, as you shall see in the continuation of the story, if you take the trouble to read it, he is only in the habit of showing himself when his presence is violently desired.

Finally, dawn broke, and it had never seemed rosier or more cheerful to Mandanne's eyes. Among all the wishes that he had been permitted to formulate, that of being considerably more handsome, for example, in order not to run any risk of displeasing Comtesse Burgos, had never crossed his mind, no man having the desire to be other than he is, even with the opportunity of being better. On that point the devil has no bargain to conclude.

When Mandanne had shaved, arranged his hair and dressed in the latest fashion, as one used to say in the good old days, and had put a hundred francs in gold coins in each of his pockets, he went . . . to the home of the Comtesse Burgos? Not at all! For an artist, you ought to know, there is something more seductive and more irresistible than the love of beauty, than the lure of curiosity, even than hunger or duty: it is the need to know what is being said about one in the newspapers, which he pretends he never reads. Reading-rooms, as everyone knows, only survive on the profits brought in by those who never go there, most notably men of letters, painters, députés, actors and all those who have dealings with the great dark individual known as the public.

People talk about the joys of the seventh heaven, but the seventh heaven is a mere attic compared with the exceptional voluptuousness of an artist reading his eulogy while drinking his morning coffee. The gilded carvings of the café, the moldings, the arabesques and guilloched cornices, seem to his fascinated gaze to be a reflection of the Alhambra; the bread is ambrosia, the fatty cutlet exhales the perfume of all the meadows in Brittany, and even the lady at the counter is a nymph reminiscent of mythology.

Mandanne experienced that poetic and dreamlike sensation, and a thousand others, as he savored his eulogy in the headlines and columns of the newspapers. One said: *The Salon is as execrable this year as it was last year; without the masterpiece of masterpieces, the miraculous portrait by the celebrated Mandanne, it would definitely be necessary to close it and put the keys under the door.*

A painter is always secretly flattered, in the depths of his soul, to hear it said that the Salon is pitiful while he is praised. Everyone thinks that he is an exception—and in the final count, the Louvre is hideous and sublime at the same time.

Another paper expressed its opinion of our artist in these terms: *We heard a rumor that Monsieur Mandanne's painting had been refused. The jury has not yet sunk so low, thank heaven. Not only has Monsieur Mandanne's famous painting not been refused, but it is exciting everyone's admiration; it is one of those marvels that appears in the arts from time to time in order to prove to jealous nations that France still holds the scepter, and is still the classical terrain of genius. It is always to her that it is necessary to turn in matters of taste, intelligence and superiority.*

When the café's waiter came to give Mandanne change due on a twenty-franc piece for the price of breakfast, Mandanne said: "Keep it."

The waiter thought: *The man's mad!*—but he kept the sixteen francs anyway.

He was going out drunk with glory, in order to go to the Hôtel d'Armainville to the home of Comtesse Burgos, when his hand fell on a wretched little newspaper edited by one of that barefoot legion who live on theater tickets while waiting to obtain a ticket to the hospital. Mandanne scanned it indifferently, his hand on the café's brass doorknob. One line stopped him—a line that was the blade of a dagger.

Yes, it read, *we agree with the immense majority of connoisseurs and the public that Mandanne is a great, sublime portrait-painter, but we are waiting for a historical painting. Until then, we shall reserve the compliment of our admiration of Monsieur Mandanne's talent.*

That petty criticism, in a ridiculously obscure paper—was it even a criticism? that observation, rather; that simple reflection born of an extreme benevolence—caused Mandanne more pain than the thousands of compliments he had gathered over breakfast had given him pleasure.

"Oh, I'm not a painter of history! But who isn't a painter of history? I shall be one when I want to be. They reproach me for not painting history . . ."

The word *history* returned to Mandanne's lips three or four thousand times before he arrived at the Comtesse's house, which he eventually reached, and where he was received by two liveried domestics.

"Madame la Comtesse is not seeing anyone today."

"But I'm Monsieur Mandanne."

"That's different," one of the domestics replied, begging the artist to accompany him to Madame la Comtesse's apartment.

Treading carpets as thick and soft as lawns, Mandanne spent ten minutes going through vast drawing-rooms decorated with a luxury redolent with an utterly royal silence. Finally, the amplitude of the rooms diminished, each one becoming smaller than the next, but always more exquisitely ornamented, until he reached the Comtesse's boudoir.

The domestic retired respectfully.

Although it was March, the Comtesse de Burgos was clad in light muslin—so light that when she raised herself up on her elbow to greet Mandanne, the latter glimpsed the blue nuance of her silk stockings through the vaporous fabric of the Oriental robe. A Greek bonnet surmounted by a golden acorn, Chinese slippers, and shoes veritably worthy of a fairy-tale completed her delightfully eccentric costume.

The Comtesse's costume naturally indicated the mild temperature that reigned in her boudoir, an atmosphere lightly charged with the perfume of hothouse flowers, and the emanations of sachets that could be seen scattered on lemonwood shelves.

"Is this pose suitable for you?" the Comtesse asked him, without giving the artist the time that was normally wasted in gazing at the whites of his eyes, his black hair and his ruddy ears the first time people saw him.

She had negligently thrown one leg over the other, set her bonnet aside and fastened a rose between the graceful shell of her ear and the gilded tangle of her beautiful blonde hair.

"You can admire me when you've painted me," she told Mandanne, who seemed to be devoting an ecstatic slowness to placing his canvas on the easel.

I didn't imagine the Comtesse like this, Mandanne thought. *How beautiful she is! How resplendent! How marvelous!*

"Your hair is slightly untidy, Madame."

"There!" she said, passing her fingers through her hair with the insouciance of a schoolboy. She was then Aida! She was the Orient! She was Spain! She was the beautiful Comtesse Burgos!

In a more emotional voice, Mandanne said: "Your arms slightly more exposed, if you please."

"You'd prefer this?" she said, pushing her long gauze sleeves back toward her neck, and then added: "So be it! It's not too bad."

Already, an astonishing resemblance was gliding beneath the trembling fingers of the painter, and as if without his being conscious of it, a delicate but emphatic, and minutely exact, sketch was delimited by the softest and warmest colors. The Comtesse de Burgos seemed to be emerging from the depths of a cloud and gradually setting herself before Mandane's eyes, who thought himself less the author than the witness of his work.

Intoxicated by his talent, and intoxicated by his model, Mandanne said once more to Comtesse Burgos, in a more emotional voice: "Your shoulders a little less hidden, Madame."

Scarcely had he expressed this wish that the Comtesse, laughing, threw off the diaphanous fabric wrapped around her neck, and her bosom, as white as a dove in flight, and her shoulders were exposed in all their dazzling firmness to the eyes of our artist—or, we ought to say, our lover. His mind was no longer on the painting;

it was soaring around his model in decreasing spirals of fire; his hand alone, distracted and agitated, never ceased to cover the canvas with a thousand enchanted layers.

And he said to himself: *A young woman who receives me in a boudoir, in a transparent muslin skirt and a Greek bonnet, which she takes off for me, and lays her arms and shoulders bare in such unusually obliging manner, must be in love with me.*

So, quitting his easel and hurling himself at the Comtesse's feet like a madman, Mandanne exclaimed: "Madame, the work of my mind is complete; that of my heart is beginning."

"Before replying to you," said the Comtesse, with an expression that was noble without ceasing to be jovial, "I want to see my portrait. If you don't have talent, I'll have my domestics throw you out; if you have an extraordinary amount . . ."

"Look, Madame," Mandanne replied, with conscientious conceit.

"It's sublime!" cried the Comtesse de Burgos, who added: "I'm sorry, Monsieur, not to respond to the love of a man of genius like yourself, but if I had had the weakness to love an artist, I would have wanted him to be both a great painter and a great sculptor, like Michelangelo, Puget and a few others."

It would be difficult to dismiss a passion with greater delicacy and good taste.

As she bid Mandanne farewell, the Comtesse slipped ten thousand-franc banknotes into his hand.

The devil—take note, you who might one day have dealings with him—only ever gives you what you ask of him, and you'll agree that that's already a great deal. Mandanne had not asked him for worldly enjoyment, and he had completely failed to obtain it in his interview with the Comtesse de Burgos. He would have known, otherwise, that the more elevated a person is in dignity, and the more use she makes of a casual manner and familiarity with those she believes to be her inferiors, the more certain it is that, at the moment that you fall at her feet, she will crush you. Imperious creole women display themselves nakedly to their slaves.

IV

Mandanne had no sooner gone home than he said to himself, in a truly unjust fit of rage against the devil: "Is it for that, then, that I've sold him my soul? To remain a painter of portraits, and not to be either a painter of history or a sculptor like Michelangelo or Puget?"

"You'll be both, my son," replied a voice that he already knew.

"But when?" Mandanne demanded.

"Right away. Get to work."

You will observe that it is the devil's custom—and we are neither going to explain nor discuss it here—only to appear once in person. The times that follow are gradually diminishing manifestations of his individuality: soon he is a voice, as in this case, then a whisper in the ear, then an item of advice—and he ends up being no more than an abstract impulse. The latter transformations are the most dangerous, for they tend to make the purchased soul forget that it is prey to the evil spirit.

The year that followed was a series of unparalleled contentments for Mandanne. He painted history with the same success that he had painted portraits, and he produced pieces of sculpture as energetic as those created by Puget's chisel and as lifelike as those of Auguste Préault.

The beautiful Comtesse de Burgos, having no more reason to refuse her heart to Mandanne, gave him her hand. As it is the custom in Spain that the woman ennobles, Comtesse Burgos, who was Spanish, made a Comte of her illustrious husband, who was no longer called anything but the Comte de Mandanne.

Happiness is a folly. Mandanne, as happy as a king, wanted to have a palace built according to his fantasy. He brought marbles from Greece and granite from Egypt, and employed them, with the rarest of taste, in the splendid habitation in which he took up residence.

When one does not possess a palace, if one is a painter, at least one can have a studio worthy of a palace. Mandanne constructed one so great, so vast, that one could ride around it on horseback. It is inexplicable why painters, to whom silence is so necessary, generally acquire, as soon as they have a name, a determined penchant for noisy pleasures and soldierly fantasies; they become children again; they like drums, hunting horns, trumpets, rifles and yataghans. If they dared, they would demand to be addressed as "general." There is one, I believe, who adopts the title of major when abroad.

Mandanne surpassed everything previously seen in that kind of mania. In the morning, clad in an equerry's boots, he mounted a bay horse, in the evening a chestnut mare, and he often painted in a cabriolet with a groom who stood behind him on the bracket-seat holding his palette. His studio permitted that kind of painting, about which there was much talk in society. That was not all; as soon as one went into his home, a drum-roll and a volley of rifle-shots was heard, and it was not rare for a cannon to resound in the antechamber in the middle of a conversation, to announce the visit of some important individual.

The newspapers made fun of these puerile extravagances, but it is as well to say here—and we beg the reader to remember it—that Mandanne had passed from reputation to renown, and from renown to celebrity; he no longer read the newspapers, although he got them all, in contrast to his early years when he had read them all but did not receive any. What would the papers have told him? Did he not have more glory than all other painters put together? What price was refused for his works? He had no time to read, when Prussia was appealing to him loudly, when Russia had commissioned twenty fifty-foot paintings, when England had sent him a thousand pounds sterling to beg him to think about her in his spare time.

If you are wondering what role the Comtesse Burgos was playing in that Olympian festival, the answer is that she was handed down to posterity every day in different guises—which is to say that she posed for her husband, sometimes modeling as a virgin and sometimes as a bacchante; one day she lent her smooth shoulders to Venus, on another her charming face was recognizable in the midst of a group at a public drinking-fountain.

She also received frequent notes composed along the following lines: *Madame, I have seen your divine torso in Brest, in a public square, beneath the cupola of a fountain; I have come to Paris expressly to assure myself that the original is as beautiful as the copy.* On other occasions there were different notes written in these terms: *I saw you this morning, naked, beneath the features of a divine statuette. Would it be permissible for me, Madame, to see clad that which, for modesty's sake, I dare not buy?*

In sum, Mandanne squandered her so wantonly, as an image, as an allegory and as an emblem, that one day, one of his colleagues stole her from him as a reality. To conjure her up in his tearful eyes, he went from fountain to fountain, contemplating the voluptuous deltoids, femurs and torsos that he had sculpted in her image.

His anguish did not last long, although he promised himself a striking vengeance. How many women, in any case, wanted to console him! Painters are in a privileged position with regard to being loved. All women flatter themselves with the thought of being models in their eyes, and—unlike poets and novelists—they never have any need to spread wit around incessantly; they are loved gratis.

Mandanne was, therefore, loved, and loved by women of the highest society. The wives of ministers adored him simultaneously; one, in order not to name her, was the wife of the Minister of the Interior; another was the wife of the Minister of Commerce.

That double intrigue was not without its storms; those two powerful women became rivals, and then it was not a matter of which one would kill the other but of which one would most effectively dishonor the other. They both succeeded, as we shall see, and by means in which the devil lost nothing—for it's only fair not to forget him in all of this.

Twenty excellent artists had offered themselves as candidates to paint the interior of an immense church that had just been completed—to no one's great contentment, because no one wanted to see it finished. Those who had gained by it were locksmiths, roofers, gilders and, above all, the entrepreneurs who stole from all the more-or-less rascally suppliers. The twenty artists in question were perfectly worthy of painting the church in question; all of them had given proof of it, and all of them had the advantage over Mandanne of having already decorated basilicas and chapels.

Mandanne prevailed over them, however, and was given sole responsibility for covering a league of walls and two leagues of ceilings with all sorts of subjects taken from the Bible—which he had never opened. The wife of the Minister of the Interior wanted it thus. There was murmuring on high and mockery down below; people were scandalized, but the wind of fortune was blowing Mandanne's way, and he triumphed over the universal mockery.

One person who was visibly mortified and jealous was the wife of the Minister of Commerce, indignant at not having, like her rival, a basilica to give to Mandanne to paint. She could not, however, lie down under the impact of that defeat. She summoned wit to her aid, which

157

is better than anger in matters of vengeance. Her boudoir was to be decorated. What did she do? She employed so much seduction on Mandanne that she persuaded him to paint portraits of her rival on every wall of her boudoir, in all the least conjugal actions of life.

Unfortunately, the wife of the Minister of the Interior was open to this vengeance in the style of Bussy-Rabutin.[1] Here she was seen in the Bois de Boulogne, riding in a calèche with the Marquis de D***; there she was supposedly taking the waters at Bagnères, but the bath-attendant was recognizable as another even older lover. As she also had the habit of finding employment for all her lovers whose reign had ended, there was much laughter at the sight of a medallion in the background of which she was seen distributing crosses, certificates and nominations to an innumerable crowd standing on the steps of her house.

When the boudoir was finished—and Mandanne had painted it with the finesse, wit and superiority whose secret you know—the wife of the Minister of Commerce hosted a soirée to which everyone illustrious in diplomacy and the arts was invited. You can imagine how

1 Roger de Rabutin, Comte de Bussy (1618-1693) was exiled from the French court in 1659, allegedly for attending an orgy, and allegedly amused himself and his mistress while in exile by composing a scurrilous "amorous history of the French," which committed to manuscript all the scandalous gossip to which he was party. It was said to have been circulated in that form, and perhaps embellished by other hands, thus confirming his exile and disrepute. His published memoirs are not without a certain scurrility, but we can only speculate as to how much smuttier the unpublished text might have been.

the boudoir, open to initiates, was visited with curiosity, commented on malignly, and how much astonishment it caused, when rumor of it spread, to the court and everywhere else.

The rival was thunderstruck at first, but soon rallied, in order to say to Mandanne's face: "You've played an odious, infamous trick on me, but love is often nothing but a tissue of treason, cowardice and knavery. Your crime arises from the fact that you love my rival more than me. Tomorrow you might perhaps change your mind—but in the meantime, Monsieur, you have to do something for me today, and if you don't like it, I'll take back all the work that you've been commissioned to do on the church, under the pretext that you're incapable of carrying it out. I'll precipitate you morally from the height of your scaffolding . . ."

Mandanne waited, before replying, for the spirit from which he took advice on such occasions to appear to him.

"Speak, Madame," he said, finally. "I'm listening."

The devil advised him to accept what had been proposed to him.

"My rival is beautiful," she began by saying. "Very beautiful."

"As are you, Madame."

"I know. That being acknowledged, listen to me."

"Yes, Madame."

"On the immense walls of the church that, thanks to me, you've been commissioned to paint, you doubtless propose to treat subjects borrowed from the Old and New Testaments?"

"I shall not employ any others."

"Among these religious scenes, women will often be depicted who are famous for their piety, their faith, their devotion or their martyrdom. They are seen dying of thirst in deserts, under torture by fire rather than allowing the slightest stain on their chastity."

"Yes, Madame."

"Well, I want all those women to have the greatest possible resemblance of face, body and appearance to my rival; in brief, I want everyone to exclaim, on seeing each of those saints: 'But it's Madame *****! It's her!' Do you understand?"

"But Madame, all Paris will utter a cry of indignation."

"You mean a burst of laughter. Anyway, the consequences of your work don't concern you. So, choose: no church to paint, or paint it as I've told you."

"But Madame, at least guarantee me impunity after my fearful boldness, for all Paris knows full well that your rival is no saint, and that her chastity . . ."

"I can only see one way of shielding you from her husband's vengeance, and that's to have you appointed as an ambassador."

"I suppose so," said Mandanne, with the most admirable aplomb—and he had, indeed, been dreaming for some time about the political glory of Rubens, who really was an ambassador.

V

The vengeance was carried out to the letter; the features of the rival of the Minister of the Interior's wife were reproduced in all the faces of the female saints painted in the church, and they will remain there forever for the edification of the faithful. Thus, she is the one people adore in praying at the feet of all the virgins who decorate that famous basilica.

After that escapade, about which future memoirs will be much more explicit than us, Mandanne was obliged to think about realizing his desire to be an ambassador. In fact, nothing else remained for him to desire: as a member of the Institut, painter of the king and commander of almost every order, what other ambition could excite him, except that of being one of the most important individuals of his era after the king?

People certainly said: "But it's ridiculous for Monsieur le Comte de Mandanne to want to become a statesman, when he is, after all, merely an artist! How will he be able to preserve and defend the interests of a great kingdom, when he has only ever lived in salons and his studio, having never been seriously occupied in anything but training horses and courting women?"

"I tell you that I shall be an ambassador," he replied to everyone, "or I shall deprive France of the glare of my genius. I shall no longer paint for her."

As it was truly impossible to grant him what he wanted with the stubbornness of a bad-tempered child, Mandanne went to Germany, where he avenged himself, as he had promised, by painting the small number of victories that the latter nation had won over France. That gesture alone proved how worthy he was to be an ambassador.

Like all the men of genius to whom he lost nothing in enjoyment of life and self-regard, he believed himself to be persecuted, and on that basis he persecuted all his colleagues. Those who did not paint according to his theory were certain of never obtaining any employment or achieving any distinction. He said, however, that his greatest pleasure was to surround himself with young people and live in the utmost simplicity. His joy was flowers, he claimed, and his only sensuality hearing the flute played. An honest man!

It was in Germany that hazard caused him to encounter his wife, the beautiful Comtesse de Burgos, and her lover. If there was ever a man who ought to have forgiven a sin, it was assuredly him, whose entire life had been nothing but one long infidelity, but he lacked that indulgence. As his wife's lover, as we have said, was a painter, and also enjoyed some consideration, although far from being able to oppose his, Mandanne abandoned himself entirely to the impulsion of his anger.

Loved by a young heir presumptive, he used his influence to have his wife's lover arrested, tried and sentenced to horrible labor in the mines, and, by a rather witty refinement of cruelty, contrived that he be employed in extracting from the bowels of the earth the blue mineral to which Prussia has given its name. He found a diabolical pleasure in painting with the color that he owed to the effects of his vengeance. He composed several paintings which he signed: *Painted by me with the color extracted from the mines by my wife's lover.*

We have reached the most brilliant and the most decisive epoch in Mandanne's life. A favorite of the prince, he lived with him on the footing of a familiarity so extraordinary that he shared his amusements and his pleasures, ate at his table and no longer wanted to paint except for him. But if happiness, as we have said, is a folly, grandeur is a vertigo; Mandanne experienced it. Intoxicated by his high position, one day when the prince was debating a matter of the history of art with him at table, Mandanne forgot himself so far as to say: "Have Vasari's work[1] brought in—ring!"

At that order, given to the prince as if he were his domestic, the latter threw a napkin in his face. Mandanne fainted.

He was dead; an attack of apoplexy had killed him. His supreme hour had sounded; the devil had taken his soul.

VI

When he woke up, Mandanne, who did not know whether he had really lived or merely dreamed, found himself in Paris, in his mansard, in front of his gigantic refused painting, *Time Discovering Truth*.

One thing, however, told him that what he had experienced had not been a dream, and that was that he was fifty years old; he had wrinkles; white hair covered his temples, and his famous painting had become blanched and yellowed.

"So I haven't been the foremost painter of my era?" he asked one of his colleagues, however—who shook his

---

1 Giorgio Vasari's *Le Vite de'più excelenti pittori, scultori, ed architettori* (1550; expanded 1568; tr. as *The Lives of the most Eminent Painters, Sculptors and Architects*).

head sadly, as one replies to a madman who asks you for an account of the past. "What! I haven't been the lover, and then the husband, of the beautiful Comtesse Burgos? Nor have I been commander of all the orders, favorite of the royal prince of Germany, the fortunate lover of the two loveliest women of my epoch?"

"It's possible, my friend," his colleague replied, "but it's necessary to work."

Mandane sighed, and stationed himself in front of his easel. Instead of the broad and tempestuous verve, the impetuosity that once he had not even had to direct, however, he felt the restraint of prudence, the embarrassment of doubt; he dared not take any risks. He did not draw a curve without wondering whether it was well-designed. Wanting, like all timid minds, to have a foot in all theories, he applied himself to reproducing all of them. And how willing he was to listen to all advice! How obedient to criticism he was! "It's necessary to draw," he said to himself, incessantly, "to draw, always to draw, and nothing but. Oh, the ancients—how they drew!"

That conduct, so opposed to what he had done before his death, had the result that he took two years to paint a portrait that was devoid of resemblance, and he spent five years relentlessly retouching his painting of *Time Discovering Truth*, which was refused six times at the Salon. He asked all the journalists for articles, and not one said anything about him.

Finally, when he was past sixty, still devoid of a name, a single commission or a single painting sold, he decided to go to America.

The only way he was able to make a living in America, was to stop in public squares or the middle of some

Indian village and unroll his painting of *Time Discovering Truth*; someone would eventually give him a handful of rice, and he would go on.

Exhausted by fatigue, hunger and discouragement, he fell down one day in front of his painting with the intention of not getting up again. He was going to die.

A Frenchman was just passing by; that Frenchman, his compatriot, who was a man of considerable intelligence, since he was traveling in America in order not to read the speeches made in the Chambre des Députés, hastened to help Mandanne. He lifted him up, and reanimated the poor old man. Suddenly, he exclaimed: "Aren't you the famous Mandanne?"

"So I have been famous!" the moribund said. "It's not a lie, an error! I've had a studio as big as a palace! I've possessed a marble palace, horses, titles! I'm not mad, then? It's really me who sold his soul to the devil."

When the Frenchman had restored some strength to Mandanne with an excellent diner, he said to him: "I can tell you that you haven't sold your soul to the devil, although it's not entirely possible for me to assure you that you haven't had some mental aberration."

"Then that prosperity..."

"It's that very prosperity that has troubled your intelligence somewhat."

"But how is it that, although once famous, adored, borne into the clouds, I've fallen into this oblivion, this poverty, this dilapidation?"

"This is why: so long as you blindly obeyed the impulsion of your genius, so long as you only listened to yourself while you were working, without paying any

165

heed to the world, uncaring about criticism, you rose up, you made progress, and you grew. People believed in you, praised you, rewarded you, made you a king; but from the day—unhappy day!—when you solicited advice, bent your ear and your knee, exaggerated the respect one owes to the past and yielded to criticism, you became a slave, you fell, and were passed over.

"The secret in the arts—why haven't you always understood this?—is to believe oneself infinitely superior to everyone else, and to have the useful common sense to declare oneself inferior to everyone else."

"Criticism doesn't exist, then?"

"Undoubtedly it exists, just like the plague—but it's necessary to guard against its infection . . . just like the plague."

"But what about the devil?"

"The devil, my dear Mandanne, is our imagination."

THE DEVIL'S SONATA

by S. Henry Berthoud

THERE was once a musician in Augsbourg named Niéser, who was equally skilled at making instruments, composing tunes and playing them; his reputation still extends throughout the region of Swabia. It is true that he was immensely rich, and that does no harm to artistes, even the most skillful ones. His less fortunate colleagues sometimes said that his opulence had been achieved by less than honorable means, but he had friends who were able to reply that those were nothing but the words of the envious.

Niéser's only heir was a daughter whose innocence and beauty would have appeared to be a sufficient dowry, even without the attractive prospect of her father's possessions. Esther was no less celebrated for the softness of her blue eyes, the grace of her smile and a thousand amiable qualities than old Niéser was for his riches, the perfection of his instruments and his prodigious talent.

Now, in spite of old Niéser's fortune and the consideration that he drew from it, and in spite of his musical celebrity, he was tormented by a great chagrin. Esther, his only child, the sole representative of a musical family extending over generations, could scarcely distinguish one note from another, and it was a source of painful reflection to Niéser not to be able to leave an inheritor of his talents, which he held in equal esteem to his wealth. As Esther grew up, however, he consoled himself with the idea that, if he could not be the father of a family of musicians, he might at least be the grandfather of one.

In fact, as soon as his daughter was old enough to marry, he made the singular resolution to give her, with a dowry of two hundred thousand florins, to the man who composed the best sonata and was best able to play it. His determination was immediately published throughout the town and the day fixed for the competition. It was even said that Niéser had affirmed on oath that he would keep his promise, even if the sonata were composed and played by the Devil himself. Perhaps it was only a joke, but it would have been better for old Niéser never to have said those words. It was obvious, some said, that he was a wicked man, with no respect for religion.

As soon as the musician's resolution was known in Augsbourg, the entire town was in a stir. Several people who had never before dared to raise such high ambitions presented themselves without hesitation as competitors for Esther's hand; for, independently of her charms and Niéser's florins, their reputation as artistes was at stake, and where there was a lack of talent, vanity stood in for it.

In brief, there was not a musician in Augbourg who did not hasten, for one reason or another, to enter the lists of which beauty was the prize. Morning, noon and night the streets of Augsburg resounded with melodious chords. At every window the sounds of a sonata in progress could be heard; there was no longer any other topic of conversation in the town than the imminent competition and its probable result. A musical fever reigned over all social classes; favorite tunes were repeated by instruments or voices in every house in Augsbourg; sentinels hummed sonatas at their posts; shopkeepers beat time on their counters with their yardsticks and their customers, when they came in, forgot what they had come to buy in order to join in. It was even said that the priests were murmuring allegros as they emerged from the confessional, and that a few bars of a rather pacy movement had been found sketched on the reverse of the bishop's homily.

In the midst of all that agitation, however, one single man remained unafflicted by the general epidemic. That was Franz Gortlingen. With as little disposition for music as Esther, he had the most noble character and was reputed to be one of the best-dressed cavaliers in Swabia. Franz loved the musician's daughter, and the latter, for her part, would have preferred hearing her name pronounced by Franz, with a few amiable compliments, to the most beautiful sonatas ever composed between the Rhine and the Oder.

On the eve of the great musical competition, Franz had not yet attempted anything for the accomplishment of his desires. How could he have done so? He had never composed a note of music in his life. To sing a simple tune to the accompaniment of a harpsichord was the *nec plus ultra* of his science.

169

That evening, Franz came out of his apartment and went down to the street. The shops were closed and the town entirely deserted. A few lights were still burning in windows, however, and the sound of instruments being prepared for the struggle that might deprive Franz of Esther struck his ears sadly. Sometimes he stopped to listen, and was even able to distinguish, through the panes, the faces of musicians satisfied with the success of their efforts and animated by the hope of triumph.

Gortlingen wandered at random, so that he eventually found himself in a part of the town that seemed entirely unfamiliar to him, although he had spent his entire life in Augsbourg. He could no longer hear anything but the roar of the river. Then, suddenly, the distant chords of a supernatural harmony reminded him once again of all his anxieties. A light coming from an isolated house proved that the reign of sleep was not yet general. Gortlingen assumed, judging by the direction of the sound, that some musician was still preparing for the next day's ordeal.

Gortlingen went on, and as he came closer to the light, such brilliant bursts of harmony were launched into the air that, ignorant as he was of music, the chords exercised a charm upon him that increasingly aroused his curiosity. He moved forward rapidly, without making any noise, all the way to the window. It was open, and inside, an old man was sitting at a harpsichord with a manuscript in front of him. His back was to the window, but an antique mirror allowed Gorlingen to see the musician's face and movements.

He had an expression of infinite gentleness and benevolence: a physiognomy of which Gortlingen could not remember ever having seen the like, but which one could have desired to see often. The old man was playing with marvelous expression; he stopped from time to time in order to make a few changes to his manuscript, and when he had appreciated their effect, he testified his joy in words that were incomprehensible, and resembled gestures of thanks, but in an unknown language.

To begin with, Gortlingen could hardly contain his indignation at the thought that that little old man might dare to present himself as one of Esther's suitors, but as he watched him and listened to him he sensed himself becoming reconciled to him by virtue of his singularly gentle physiognomy, and also by the beauty and particular character of his music.

Finally, at the conclusion of a brilliant passage, the artiste perceived that he was not alone, for Gortlingen, no longer able to restrain his admiration, had stifled the moderate exclamations of the old man with his applause. Immediately, the old man got up and opened the door.

"Good evening, Herr Franz," he said. "Sit down and tell me how you like my sonata, and whether you think it can win the prize."

There was something benevolent in the old man's face, something soft in his voice. Gortlingen felt all jealousy disappear, and he listened.

"Does my sonata please you?" said the old man, as he finished.

"Alas!" replied Gortlingen. "If I were only capable of doing as much!"

"Listen to me," said the old man. "Niéser has made a criminal oath in swearing that he would give his daughter to whoever composes the best sonata, even if it were the Devil himself, and played by his hand. Those words have been heard, and repeated by the echo of the forests, have been carried on the wings of the wind and night all the way to the ears of the one who dwells in the valley of darkness; the Demon's cries of joy burst forth. But the genius of good was alert; so, without taking pity on Niéser, the fate of Ester and Gortlingen has touched him. Take this score; go into Niéser's drawing-room; a stranger will present himself to dispute the prize; two others will seem to be accompanying him: the sonata I have given you is the same one that they will play, but mine has a particular virtue: watch for an opportunity, and substitute this one for his."

After this extraordinary speech, the old man took Gortlingen by the hand; he led him through unfamiliar streets to one of the gates of the city, and left him.

As he returned home with his scroll of paper, Gotingen lost himself in his reflections regarding that bizarre adventure and conjectures relating to the next day's event. There had been something in the old man's physiognomy that he could not mistrust, and yet it was impossible for him to comprehend how he could obtain any advantage from the substitution of one sonata for another, since he was not one of the suitors for Esther's hand. He went up to his room and went to bed. While he was asleep, Esther's image danced before his eyes, and the old man's sonata resonated in the air.

The next day, at sunset, the Niéser house was opened to the competitors. All the musicians of Augsbourg were then seen, hurrying there with scrolls of paper in hand, while a crowd gathered at Niéser's gate to watch them pass by.

When the time had come, Gortlingen, taking his score, also went to Niéseer's door. All those who knew him felt sorry for him, because of his love for the musician's daughter; they said to one another: "What's Franz doing with that paper in his hand? Surely he isn't thinking of entering the lists? Poor fellow!"

When he entered the room, Gortlingen found it full of suitors and the music-lovers of Augsbourg, who had been invited to the session. When Gortlingen crossed the room with his musical score, smiles appeared on the faces of the musicians, who all knew one another, and also knew that he could hardly play a march, much less a sonata, even if he were able to compose one. On seeing him, Niéser smiled too, but when Esther's eyes met his, he was seen to wipe away a tear.

It was announced that the rivals could come forward to inscribe their names, and that the order of play would be decided by lot. The last to present himself was a stranger, for whom everyone made way as if by instinct. No one had seen him before and no one knew where he had come from. His physiognomy was so repulsive and there was something so extraordinary about his gaze that even Niéser could not help whispering to his daughter that he hoped that that man's sonata would not be the best.

"Let's begin the trial," said Niéser. "I swear to give my daughter, whom you can see sitting beside me, with a dowry of two hundred thousand florins, to the man who composes the best sonata and can play it most perfectly."

"And you'll keep your word!" said the stranger, advancing to face Niéser.

"I'll keep my word," said the musician of Augsbourg, "even if the sonata is composed by the Devil in person and played by him."

Everyone fell silent and shivered; only the stranger smiled.

The first name presented by the ballot was that of the stranger, who immediately took his place and unrolled his score. Two men whom no one had noticed previously placed themselves by his sides with their instruments, awaiting the signal to begin. All eyes were upon them. The signal was given, and when the three musicians raised their heads to follow the music, everyone perceived, with horror, that their faces were similar.

A frisson ran through the audience. No one dared speak to his neighbor, but people began to draw their cloaks more tightly about them and slip silently away. Soon, the entire audience had disappeared, with the exception of the three who were continuing to play the sonata and Gortlingen, who had not forgotten the old man's advice. Old Niéser was still in his seat, but he was trembling at the memory of his fatal oath.

Gortlingen was standing close to the musicians; as they approached the finale, he boldly substituted his paper for theirs. An infernal grimace contracted the faces of the three artistes, and a distant groan resounded like an echo.

A few hours after midnight, the old man was seen leading Esther and Gortlingen out of the room, but the sonata was still continuing.

The years went by. Esther and Gortlingen were married, and reaching the end of their lives; the strange musicians, however, were still pursuing their task, and old Niéser, it is said, was still sitting in his seat, beating time.

SINCERITY

by Jules Janin

IF one exercises the profession of *belles-lettres* with a certain zeal, it is necessary not to neglect anything. Everything is of use, or might be of use. Who would have thought that, in an old collection of Latin sermons, devoid of a date but which reeks of the distance of the sixteenth century, a nameless Dominican would have collected, in the manner of *Sermones discipuli de tempore*,[1] two hundred and twelve dramatic stories for all the Sundays and principal festivals of the year? "I have called these sermons 'The Sermons of a Neophyte' because there is nothing magisterial in these innocent stories, and any schoolboy might have written them, or made them up." With the result that young preachers, when they want to keep their audience attentive, will only have to dip their hands into these tales, whose entire merit is in their naivety.

---

1 *Sermones discipuli et tempore* (1418) is a famous collection made by the Dominican preacher Johann Herolt, also known as Discipulus. Herolt also collected exemplary stories for use in sermons, similarly circulated in manuscript and widely reprinted as *Promptuaria exemplorum*.

That said, the Dominican gets down to business, and from among those storiettes, we have chosen the present story of the Devil and the bailiff.

The bailiff in question was the scourge of a dozen unfortunate villages in the Jura, grouped around a wretched fortified château, where devastation, conflagration and war had left their formidable imprint.

People had been breathing sadness in that desolate region for a long time; if one were searching for the worst possible place to reside, the cleverest individual could not have found anything more propitious than that heap of sufferings and ennuis. Nature herself, in her most charming beauties, had been vanquished by tyrannical force.

In that desolate place, the echoes had forgotten the refrains of songs; the somber woods were inhabited by silent guests; the osprey and the vulture were the sole inhabitants of those Northern firs whose savage cries were heard. On the shores of depopulated lakes no frogs croaked. The livestock went hungry; the errant bee had been chased away, poor thing, from her smoked-out hive.

There were no more paths in the fields, no more bridges over the streams, not a single barge on the river. There was still a banal mill, but no bread for the oven. It was said, however, that the villagers had once cooked buckwheat galettes in that oven, and that, on days before festivals, a little meat at the bottom of a covered dish— but the dish had been broken.

Fire and plague had been the only distractions of those dolorous houses. The militia had taken away the strong, fever had carried away the young. A few old people still remained to utter curses.

The devouring hyena and the wolf had passed through the cemetery. The church was empty; the bell no longer rang for want of a rope, with which the provost, for the sake of economy, had hanged the most unfortunate. That was the sole charity that the poor could expect.

Thus, of the Lord above and the lord below, there was not a trace. In vain it is written: "No land without a lord, and no Heaven without a god!" It was true, however: God was no longer there! The Marquis de Mondragon, the absolute master of the seigneury in question, was absent; his wife no longer came to the place, and his children no longer came.

Shame and dishonor had preceded that ruin. Oh, there was nothing but rags to cover that man's vassals, and nothing but wild plants to nourish them. The leeches had scarcely left those poor folk a little flesh stuck to their bones. Woe unto them! For such a long time they had supported the men of war, the men of business, the king's men, princes of the blood, officers of the crown and gentlemen in His Majesty's service—so many birds of prey and plunderers.

In the end, when they had been visibly reduced to nothing, the kings, princes, lords, captains and the marquis seemed to have forgotten that that little corner of earth existed. That was a release, and the race in question, taxed and worked to exhaustion, might perhaps have ended up finding a little hope and a few ears of corn, if Monsieur le Marquis had not left his bailiff behind in his devastated marquisate.

With a little more courage, the bailiff in question might have been a man-at-arms in the service of some provincial ravager. He had not become a man of war because he had not dared to carry a torch or wield a sword. He had given himself the unique task, having the right of low and high justice for ten leagues around, and being the sovereign judge, to leave nothing in the hovels: not a single egg, or wisp of cloth, or loaf of bread, or bundle of straw. He came back from every expedition carrying something, and suspecting his peasants of hiding their money and their livestock. Four times a year that torturer set out on campaign—and every man for himself!

Now, one somber and rainy day in autumn, at a time when the north wind and winter were already advancing, the bailiff of the Sires de Mondragon emerged from the château, warmly wrapped up in the cloak of an unfortunate farmer that he had sent to the galleys. Two serfs followed him, carrying empty sacks. He was mounted on his horse, well-nourished on oats and hay—such good oats that the Christians of the regions would have baked bread for their wedding-feasts with them.

The sight of that man was terrible. He advanced, however, at a careful pace in the solitude and the silence. He understood that hatred was at his heels, and that vengeance went before him—but nothing stopped him in these supreme expeditions.

When he had gone past the cemetery and the church, at a bend in the road, he entered a heath as sterile as all the rest, and went into a stand of old trees that it was absolutely necessary to go through before reaching the villages of the seigneury. Not encountering anyone, he had gradually begun to feel reassured, when he saw a man—or, at least, a phantom—step out from behind an old oak whose top was lost in the sky, and place his powerful hand on the horse's rump.

A tremor ran through the horse's entire body. Then the rider, turning his head, dared to look his silent companion in the face.

He was not so much a body as an image, a shadow. Two implacable black eyes were shining in his face; even their whites were black. They were shining, menacing and burning.

The bailiff had no difficulty in recognizing that he had just met his godfather, the Devil, in person.

The other said to him, in an unearthly voice: "I know where you're going, and I'm going the same way. Let's travel together."

They were going on in that fashion when they saw, at a crossroads in the forest—it's incredible, but it's true—a peasant leading a pig, coming back from an acorn-hunt. By that miraculous means, he had saved the pig, and was taking it back home, trembling lest he be spotted by one of the bailiff's assessors.

Certainly, the latter would not have liked anything better than to put the animal in a sack and go back to the château, to set out on campaign again the next day; but the horse was obedient to the tenebrous hand. At the same time, the pig refused to go any further, and started struggling with all its might.

"May the Devil take you!" cried the peasant.

At these words, the bailiff, who was beginning to tremble forcefully, felt entirely reassured, because it is customary among the demons of the other world, and the demons of this one, that as soon as the Devil has found his prey, he must necessarily accept it and go away, in search of another adventure.

Thus, if you encounter Satan himself, you can give him to take away the first creature that is offered to his eyes. "Agreed!" Satan will say. Then he will have to be content with a black hen, or a sheep, or even less—a frog in the middle of the road. These sorts of pacts, however, don't displease him, because hazard and Satan are good friends. More than once he has encountered the old father, or the wife, or the son of the same companion, who has thought that he has got out of it cheaply.

Alas, it's the story of Iphigenia or Jephthah's daughter.[1]

So, the bailiff, his little eyes radiant with cunning, said to the black eyes: "Since it's been given to you, friend phantom, take your prey and go away. Well, what are you waiting for? That's the pact, and I'm saved from your claws."

To which the black man replied with silent laughter, and little blue flames emerged from his mouth. "Yes," he said, "I'll take the prey that I've been given, and I'll leave you, unless, of course, this gentleman hasn't given me his pig sincerely. It's the sincerity that makes the gift, as you know. It's not a matter of saying something; it's necessary that the intention should be wholehearted. Let's wait."

As he spoke, the Devil and the bailiff saw a dozen charcoal-burners coming through the wood, who, on

---

1 The story of Jephthah's unwise promise to sacrifice the first creature he meets after returning home from defeating the Ammonites is told in *Judges* 11. The most familiar versions of the story of Agamemnon's sacrifice of his daughter Iphigenia, as told by Homer and Euripides, do not introduce a similar twist to the story.

seeing the pig coming in their direction, uttered cries of joy.

"Oh, my God!" they said. "Where did you find so much fodder, friend Jean?" And they surrounded the animal and its guide. They could not contain their joy. They danced around, singing: "Friend pig! What a feast and what joy! We'll eat your blood, we'll eat your flesh! We'll make chops, sausages and black puddings; your head and trotters will give us relief from a long fast!"

And they were all so contented, so joyful, that they did not even see the bailiff. The latter went on his way.

"As you see," his comrade said to him, with a malevolent snigger, "those starving peasants hadn't given me the pig sincerely."

The bailiff lowered his head, wondering what the Prince of Darkness was getting at. He knew that, of all the logicians of the Aristotelian school, the Devil was the greatest. There was no argument that he could not twist, no syllogism in which he could not immediately find a fault.

Meanwhile, they arrived at the door of a hut, and on the threshold they found a humble old woman who was spinning with her distaff and agitating a little crib with her weary foot. The baby was crying and moaning, calling for his mother; he was hungry. The mother had gone out to collect dead branches, and the baby was crying incessantly.

"Oh, accursed child," said the old woman, "may the Devil take you!"

At this, the wicked bailiff conceived a glimmer of hope again. The old woman was so poor! One child more in that hovel was one mouth more! The miserable bailiff imagined that toil had reduced those men and women to be nothing more than savage beasts of the woods.

One might have thought that his colleague with the cloven hoofs was of the same opinion. Already, he was reaching out his hand to take possession of the frail jetsam, and when that was done, the Devil would be vanquished . . .

But as soon as the shadow had touched the crib, the old woman, whose arms were still vigorous, carried the baby away to her mother, who had just arrived, laden with branches, singing: "Mister Wolf, don't listen, get thee gone/A mother can hear her crying son."

"You're here, at last, my daughter!" cried the grandmother. "The child's calling for you—he's thirsty and hungry, and I can't rock him any more."

The young mother, throwing down her burden, uncovered her breast and showed it to the child, who began to smile.

"Oh, I pity you," said the Demon to his companion. "You can see that I acted in good faith, but you can't maintain that the old woman had given me her little child with a good grace. Come on, courage! Let's look for something else. We still have a way to go before we get down to your business. But it's good to hear the words of that song; it's an old tale from before my time."

And they went on their way.

The further they went, the darker the sky became, and yet noon had not yet sounded. They were going between two hedges, the bailiff thinking about his destiny and searching his arsenal for some ruse, the Devil murmuring an old song derisively. The two sack-bearers were perfectly indifferent to everything that was happening around them, for their humble condition sheltered them from the anger of the Prince of Darkness.

One might have thought that the solitude had magnified and that the road was growing longer of its own accord. There was no sadder sight than those four monotonous travelers.

There was, however, an unexpected bright spot: a new house of cheerful appearance. It was built in good stone and covered with tiles, and with lattice windows—very rare in those days—that were glittering in the sunlight. One might have thought that the masterpiece in question had been brought to the hillside ready-made during the night, for exhibition to the rising sun. A great ease and excellent order presided over the habitation. A vigilant cockerel could be heard crowing; dogs were yapping; a beautiful cow with full udders was wandering freely in the thick grass. Pigeons could be heard cooing on the roof, and ducks splashing in the pond, and vines were running over a trellis alongside the vegetable garden.

The Demon contemplated such great abundance without envy, and turned to the astounded bailiff. "My opinion, Master Cut-throat, is that here's a dwelling neglected by your procedures. Beware, lest I tell your master—doubtless he'll throw out an accountant as negligent as you."

The bailiff did not know what to say. He was both happy to have discovered this new subject of mortmain and ashamed of not having exploited such fortune before. He was so covetous of it that he forgot his companion momentarily. Finally, and having made sure that he had his ink-pot and parchment bearing the lord's watermark—it was a broken pot, a telling image of feudalism—he looked for an open door in order to institute proceedings against a vassal bold enough to be a little better lodged than his seigneur.

The doors were closed, but the window was open, and from the height of his horse the bailiff was able to contemplate at his ease the crimes contained in that honest house.

The first crime was a beautiful walnut table, covered with a white cloth, and on the cloth—O forfeit!—a loaf of white bread, and white salt in a salt-cellar; a joint of venison on a rich pewter tray, shinier than silver, announced a meal such as had been eaten before the crusade under Saint Louis. Two silver goblets were filled to the brim with vermilion liquid. A tankard carved by a master, and beautiful plates representing the king and queen of France, added their splendor to all those bourgeois riches. The furniture was not unworthy of everything else.

Finally, two young people, a husband and wife, in all the gleam of youth and strength, were sitting there, surrounded by three beautiful children dressed like princes, and doubtless not very hungry, to see them laughing and chattering to one another.

As the bailiff's eyes devoured that meal, which an ancient knight errant would have found cooked to perfection, and as he was already making an inventory of that suspect wealth, a sharp and loud argument suddenly broke out between the husband and the wife. It seemed that the latter had bought, without telling the former, a gold necklace from the neighboring town, and the husband was reproaching her for the expense.

After the first skirmish, they very rapidly came to angry words, to finish up with these, so full of danger:

"To the Devil with you, Wife!"

"To the Devil with you, Husband!"

At that moment, we can agree that the temptation was great even for the Devil, and that the prey was luscious. A wife of twenty, a husband of almost the same age: to carry them away immediately would represent a good diabolical day's work.

"What's stopping you, friend?" said the bailiff to his comrade. "Where will you find two such beautiful souls, and more tears than those in the eyes of the three children? Play your part; I'll play mine; and we'll part as good friends."

All seemed lost, therefore. The bailiff was triumphant; the beautiful house trembled to its foundations. The children were weeping. The mother and father were damned . . .

But in the depths of their souls, they loved one another too much to be at odds with one another for long.

"What have you've done, my darling?" cried the young man, throwing his arms around his wife. "What have you done? I'm a wretch for having scolded you for so little! A thread of gold! To reproach you for a thread of gold, when I ought to have covered you in diamonds and pearls!"

"No, no!" cried the young wife, with large tears in her eyes. "It's my fault, not yours. Why, indeed, have I had so little heart as to spend our children's dowry on vanities?"

Then, quitting her husband's embrace, she kissed the two little boys and the beautiful little girl ardently, the children no longer knowing whether to laugh or to cry. And when, finally, all five of them wiped away those soft tears and found their smiles again, they placed the little necklace on the Madonna's head, by way of an *ex-voto*, and all five of them knelt down before the divine mother, and recited, with their hands joined: "Hail Mary, full of grace!"

At this point the Devil felt so touched that a tear escaped from his eye and trickled down his cheek. A *pssst!* was heard: the sound of a drop of water falling on a hot stove.

The bailiff was not in the least touched. He felt his fury increase, and not for anything would he have retraced his steps—but with the Devil, it is always necessary to go forward. He is the voice that says: "Forward march! One, two!"

In vain you want to call a halt in some beautiful part of the enchanted land. "Forward march! One, two!" In vain the city offers its singular beauties to your eyes. "Forward march! One, two!" In vain the libertine requests a moment of respite to quit his bad mores and marry some innocent. "Onwards! Forward march! One, two!" There are even moments in which the traitor and the tyrant would gladly call a truce in their criminal maneuvers. "Forward march! You've let repentance pass. Arrive, limping, at the punishment that will claim you!" Thus, too, go the ambitious man, when he renounces ambition, the miser when he renounced money, the soldier when he renounces murder and the debauchee when he renounces his daily pleasures: "Forward march! One, two!"

It is necessary to obey, all the way to the yawning abyss. It is necessary.

So the bailiff marched. Nevertheless, as he was cunning and a past master in devilry himself, he said to his companion: "It's my right to go forward along the road I choose."

"That's your right," the other replied, "incontestably."

With which the bailiff, reassured, took a little path over the mountain.

That path lengthened the journey by a full league, and the Devil—who is quite easily caught out—had a suspicion that the bailiff was playing a trick on him. "Are you setting a trap for me?" he said. "Let us, as they say, put our cards on the table, and let each of us be content."

"Everyone has his turn, Monseigneur," the bailiff replied. "You had me a little while ago, and now I have you. Incompetent! It wasn't worth the trouble of running all over the country and setting all those traps for me, only to fall into my ambush! Where are we, at present, comrade? Don't you see that we've taken the path that leads to the convent of Sainte-Croix? The convent has disappeared—I'm the one who razed it, and I took possession of all its domains—but I respected the calvary, raised on these heights on the very day of the Passion, and that calvary contains the relics of Saint Peter the Martyr, Saint Eutropius, Saint Bartholomew, Saint Catherine, virgin and martyr, and ten thousand crucified martyrs. That's where I'll wait for you, Messire Demon, and we'll see whether you dare pursue me into the shadow of the cross.

Who was irritated by this declaration? It was Satan. He was annoyed with himself for having forgotten the formidable rampart that the saints had erected with their pious hands on the mountain. He was aware, moreover, of the strength and authority of certain relics buried in that calvary. Finally, he was annoyed with himself for having been duped by a bailiff of the worst sort, and for having met someone more cunning than himself. It was his battle of Pavia.[1]

I'll get my revenge another time, he said to himself, sulkily. However, as he did not want to go away empty-handed, he said to the bailiff: "I'll go to seek my fortune elsewhere, if you'll at least give me those two scoundrels marching behind you. Is that agreed?"

"You won't get them from me," said the bailiff, flicking a yellow tooth with a fingernail. "Those two men are necessary to my high and low justice. One is the executioner of our domains. No one knows better than he does how to whip a rebel with bloody rods, to brand a poacher with a hot iron marked with two fleurs-de-lys, or to rivet a chain around the neck of a convict destined to row His Majesty's galleys in perpetuity. The other is the concierge of our prisons and the executor of our sentences; he excels in hanging insolent debtors, and has put substantial sums into our coffers more than once. It's impossible for me to do without either of them. So go back whence you came with empty hands, and good night, Master Demon."

---

1 At the battle of Pavia in 1525, François I was defeated by the Spaniards and taken prisoner; he subsequently wrote to his mother: "Madame, all is lost, except honor."

As he spoke, they were already half way up the mountain. The Devil was about to go when he decided to dig his heels in.

"Come on," he said, laughing ominously, "at least let's promise to spare one of those wretches?"

"Not one," said the bailiff. "They've caused me too much trouble this morning."

"At least spare the residents of that new house!"

"Oh, their account's drawn up. I'll have the gold necklace in my pocket this evening, and if you come back this way a month hence, the entire area will be covered by brambles and stubble."

"But the little baby at the teat!"

"He'll pay for his mother's milk!"

"And the pig?"

"My acolytes and I will eat it this evening."

"In sum, neither pardon nor pity?"

"Neither pity nor . . ."

At this point, the bailiff's voice catches in his throat. He is looking hard, but he can no longer see the calvary. In vain, his interrogative gaze searches in every direction. The holy cross that ought to protect him is not there.

"Yes, indeed," said Satan. "You're searching in vain for your strength and your support. The unfortunates that you've created have felled the calvary. By dint of poverty, they've ceased to hope and believe. Insensate! There are the ruins that your malice and cowardice ought to have foreseen. Those desperate folk have taken their revenge on the relics of the martyrs, and now it's you who'll be punished for the profanations of all those unfortunates."

At that revelation, whose justice he understood fully, the bailiff fell off his horse, and the horse, relieved of its double burden—the man and the Devil—ran off at a gallop, striking up such a firework display, with so many sunbursts, bombs and rockets, that it would have been enough to celebrate the birthday of the greatest king in the world.

Seeing the man crushed by shame and fear, Satan raised him gently to his feet, as an affectionate father might have done for his only son, and all four of them went down the gentle slope that led to the various villages of that abominable seigneurie.

They went past the first houses, without hearing anything but moans and tears—but no curses, as yet. The people were afraid, trembling in their every limb. The sick held their breath and children put down their toys; frightened women went to hide in some covert, and the dogs forgot to bark. Finally, however, when they had traveled the length of an entire street, they heard murmurs, cries, plaints and maledictions emerging from the debris of the cottages. The unanimous curse was incessant and ever-increasing.

In the second village, the neighbor of the first, anger had replaced complaint, and the unfortunates were crying:

"Down with the brigand who has stolen my son!"

"Death to the blackguard who caused my father to perish under the rod!"

"There's the pitiless monster!"

And the children threw stones at the infernal sinner.

"Give us back our bread!" said the women.

"Give us back our honor!" said the men. "Give us back our beds and our cribs! Look—famine is undermining us, and our feeble hands could no longer hold the implements that you have stolen from us!"

At that immense racket, in which teeth were grinding and eyes blazing, in which those meager and desiccated torsos emitted hoarse cries and feverish whistles, villagers of both sexes came running, and as their vengeful fingers pointed at the impious man, they all shouted: "To the Devil! To the Devil! To the Devil!"

And the echoes repeated: "To the Devil! To the Devil!"

Then Satan, in a voice that filled the plain and the mountain, said: "Comrade, it's agreed that I will only accept a gift made with a good grace, and with one voice, without any of the donors wanting to retract it. Well, how does this seem to you? What do you say to this unanimous malediction? Now you're mine, well and truly mine. Not one of them is claiming you or forgiving you."

And, picking up the bailiff by the shoulders, he suspended him from an oak that was no less than sixty feet high.

The entire country applauded that act of vengeance! Alas, for want of justice, one takes revenge, and that is why it is necessary to be just before all else.

The man in question having disappeared from the domain, order and peace were gradually seen to return to the region.

The church was rebuilt, and the bell once again called the faithful to prayer; they obeyed the sacred summons, precisely because they had ceased to be miserable.

The men returned to the plough, to the harrow and to all the instruments that give life and enjoyment to humankind.

The pig, saved by a miracle, had an abundant progeniture.

The little baby grew up and became a great dispenser of justice, the leader of a parliament whose voice was sovereign.

No one was astonished when, one morning, the old château was disemboweled, its materials used to build an aqueduct, a bridge and a highway.

Finally, you will have guessed that the new lord was the young man from the new house.

They had begun by renouncing their right to the scaffold, their right to the galleys and the gibbet; they had converted the scaffold into a signpost to guide travelers in the forest.

We have one more adventure to relate, and all will be said. On the day when the bailiff disappeared, the elders of the village who had maintained their composure had clearly seen that Satan, his hands full of lightning-bolts, had engraved something unknown on the highest branch of the old oak. The old oak died of old age, and the woodcutters, when they stripped it of its crown, found a memorable word written in streaks of fire:

JUSTICE!

A WOMAN IN HELL

by Lucie Delarue-Mardrus

WE are still far from knowing everything that exists in the simple terrestrial world, even though we are already anxious about the mores of the Moon, not to say Mars. However, it has been revealed to us, among other secret particularities of our planet, that somewhere in the open sea—no one knows in what latitude—there is an island unknown to geography that has been exclusively populated, since the earliest days of the world, by a colony of devils.

Do they constitute a reserve on which Providence can draw when it wants to provoke modern cases of possession? They must be, in any case, similar to the slightly comical but very dangerous kinds of demons that have beards and goat's horns, and spread a sulfurous odor when they move.

We can imagine very nearly the mode of existence of those satanic islanders, which are, in any case, only satanic in the human sense of the word, when they approach some strange creature, and among themselves, they are not harmful or frightening, all being of the same species.

They believe that the world ends at the limits of their

marine solitude. They are utterly unaware of the existence of men and women. However, a vague tradition, a sort of informal liturgy has remained in their race since the epoch of the Old Testament. They know that events took place in remote times, in the course of which they, the devils, were plagued—and yet they have lost the magnificent name of Lucifer, and even, in addition, that of God. But the imps are nevertheless able to murmur tremulously the mysterious word "angel," which they only pronounce while lowering their voice and their eyes.

Apart from that last remembrance, life, for them, has scarcely any complications. They have an absolute monarch, who is simply the strongest and wiliest member of the colony, who lives alone in a tent made of animal skins. The rest of the people are content with burrows. They walk on four feet or two, depending on the moment. They are hairy, horned and unclothed. There are phosphoric gleams in their yellow eyes with retractile pupils. Marriage does not exist, but a free union logically contained, as in animals; and when the amorous season is over, the she-devils cradle and nurse their newborns, which have the faces of Siamese cats. But maternity, for them, is merely a normal and succinct crisis, like amour; it does not encumber their entire existence.

As for the language of the island, it is evidently rudimentary, scarcely articulate, very guttural, and manifest above all by gestures.

Now, one day, a tempest disturbed the sea. That was a relatively frequent occurrence. The somber waves arrived from the horizon and broke, white, upon the rocks. The rapid clouds dipped in the water. There was rumbling at sea, and a splendid racket on land. The assaulted cliffs trembled. The rain came down violently and obliquely; the trees all inclined in the same direction, in the midst of the disarray of their overturned foliage. Such wrath filled the world that the animals were hiding in the depths of their lairs, and also the intimidated devils. No one saw the frightful spectacle of the shipwreck that occurred at sea, a few miles from the haunted coast. And in any case, who could have divined what a ship in distress signified, since no one had ever suspected the existence of humans?

But when the storm had finally eased, the next morning, while walking along the shore ravaged by the sea, a few devil fishermen perceived, lying on the sand, a white piece of wreckage like none they had seen before. They approached and, to begin with, freed it from the sand that partly covered it.

Then they recoiled in surprise and fear, for they could not explain what they had just discovered.

Was it one of their females, since it had breasts, a face and hands? And yet, its hairless body was smooth, intact and white, like the flesh of certain fish. But what upset their minds most of all was seeing, on the head of the extraordinary creature, which was deprived of horns, a kind of gigantic mane growing, so long that it could have covered its knees, the color of which resembled none of the various known furs. Positively, it emerged like light from the head . . .

A strange frisson passed through the witnesses; and suddenly, with a precise and spontaneous movement, they all fled as fast as their legs could carry them in the direction of the king's tent.

You can imagine the tumult that filled the island in a moment. The diabolical ant-hill swarms in all directions. Soon, with the king at the head, the entire population is on the shore, marching toward the fishermen's find. They look, without daring to touch, at the hands, the feet and the face; they tremble before the long blonde hair; they are ecstasized by the whiteness of the body, doubtless dead, arrived from the secret depths of the sea. And suddenly, with a prophetic cry, his claws clutching his hairy cheeks, the king looks at his frightened people and howls:

"I know what it is! It's an angel!"

Very slowly, the woman came round. The people recoiled, palpitating, gazing at her. As soon as she opened her blue eyes, such a brightness spread over the world that the hundred thousand devils of the island fell to their knees together. The vague religiosity that remained to them from their origin doubtless dictated that impulsive movement.

She spoke. It was an agile language, incomprehensible and musical. And the entire assembly, inclined like the faithful at mass at the moment of the elevation, listened to the angel finally revealed, the sublime sexless being, beautiful, white, soft and redoubtable.

The woman said: "I'm scared! I'm scared! Oh, how scared I am! I surely died in the shipwreck and all these horned devils that surround me inform me that I'm in Hell. Here I am, then damned for eternity. If I'd known, I wouldn't have sinned so much all my life!"

However, it is necessary to say that she quickly took account of that afterlife; for, soon having seen what sort of characters she was dealing with, she set out to domesticate the entire menagerie. And every day she thought: *Is this all that Hell is* . . . ?

And because women are very adaptable, she learned to eat, drink and talk like those who surrounded her. She abstained from walking on all fours, however; and that ever-upright stance continued to fascinate the king and his subjects. And then, was the blonde comet that followed her not sufficient to reveal that the creature was of the same species as the stars? When she passed by, people dropped to their knees and turned their heads away. No one dared to speak to her. They brought her food tremulously. The king had a tent similar to his own made for her, in an absolutely isolated location elevated above the sea.

At length, definitively reassured regarding her fate, the woman ended up getting bored. The infinite respect of the perverts weighed upon her. Doubtless, she would have liked, having learned their language, to approach, converse and distract herself, but as soon as she made a move toward one of them he prostrated himself in the dust or ran away screaming in fear.

However, one evening, in the amorous season, as the woman was wandering, pensive and alone, on the crepuscular edge of a cliff not far from her tent, she saw a tall devil hiding in the bushes, who appeared to be watching her. It was an adult in quest of a mate, and he had not encountered anyone since the previous day.

What sensory madness, what animal impulse, suddenly impelled that enamored male? Bounding like a jaguar from the branches that hid him, he threw himself on the angel, on the sexless being coiffed with light, and, forgetting all liturgy, threw her down in the sand brutally. And the sun, as it disappeared into the sea, splashed the contradictory couple—the couple forever symbolic of the luminous and white seraph struggling in the grip of the somber demon—with a bloody last light.

The next day, ashamed and terrified, the unfortunate adult devil, who had not slept all night, was prowling on the edge of the same cliff, in accordance with the habit of criminals who cannot help returning to the scene of their crime. His head bowed, he calculated all the consequences of his extraordinary action. Certainly, by his fault, innumerable calamities were going to rain down upon the profanatory island.

In despair, he bit his claws, one after the other. And the phosphor of his eyes brightened, red and blue, as the shadow commenced, as if two glow-worms were lodged in his skull.

When he arrived at the location of the fatal bush, he stopped dead, sensing all the hair on his body standing on end. For the angel, upright, immaculate and naked in her starry hair, was watching him come. And the miserable devil thought: *The hour of vengeance has come! What's going to happen to me now?*

His spine low, like a culpable dog, he was already sketching a prostration when he saw, with an indescribable stupor, the angel making a sign of a significance so evident and so peremptory that he could not do otherwise, in his religious obedience, than recommence the gesture of the previous evening precisely.

You can imagine that the entire island was informed of the event in a matter of days. The height of the cliff, henceforth, saw all the adult devils in the colony file past, one after another, not to mention the old men and the adolescents. The adoration of the people for their angel, although more intimate in that fashion, was only exalted further. And the she-devils, initially jealous of such rivalry, gradually succeeded—no one knows how—in reconciling themselves to it.

The king eventually heard what was happening, and as he was invested with absolute power, he immediately declared that he intended to appropriate the angel exclusively.

For the first time, there was great discord on the island. The people wanted, at any price, to keep the angel for their collective usage, but the king intended to have her exclusively to himself. Seeing that, the woman first made the people a little speech in which she promised to remain theirs, as in the past. Then, having gone to find the king outside his tent, she swore solemnly and publicly only to belong to him alone.

"But," said the hundred thousand devils in their own language, when she came back from the tent, "what will you do, O angel, in order to keep both your promises? If the king takes you for his queen, don't you know that he will always keep you with him? And even at night, at the time for sleep, he will wrap his arms around your shoulders, in such a way that, if you try to get up to come out and find us, his great black claws will enter into your skin of their own accord and perhaps wound you mortally."

But she replied to them: "Leave it to me."

For she knew that a hundred thousand rogues, with their animal cunning, their sulfurous souls and all their demonic apparatus, knew less than a simple woman, since Eve, our ancestress, as soon as the first footsteps of existence, had found a way to deceive the Eternal Father himself, although he was supposed to know everything.

So, when night fell, when the satanic king commenced to snore happily next to the woman, and his great vigilant claws surrounded her shoulders tightly, gently, by means of a series of insensible movements, she slid her naked body under the edge of the tent, in such a fashion that her upper body, still imprisoned by the dangerous claws, having faithfully remained, down to the waist, in the royal bed, the rest of her person was lying outside on the warm earth, in the starry night, where the obscure devils in love with their angel were prowling.

Thus she kept her double promise.

And so profound was the admiration of the entire colony for that streak of perversity that the following day, the demons, united in extraordinary assembly, elected the angel for their sole king. Only, as they dared not attack the legitimate throne, the seraph, by virtue of a hidden agreement, became for them a secret king, more real than the other, although not nominally recognized.

So that, by virtue of having fooled everyone, the woman mistaken for an angel found herself the absolute master in Hell, without having the title—just as among humans.

THE TRUTH ABOUT FAUST

by Maurice Renard

DOCTOR FAUST, a graying quinquagenarian, looked at his visitor thoughtfully.

Mephistopheles was sitting very comfortably in a large winged armchair, the leather of which was burning slowly, with a nauseating odor, in response to contact with his person. The Devil was tapping the arm-rests with a clawed hand, which left marks like a hot iron. He affected to be waiting, not without impatience, for the alchemist's decision, and scanned the surroundings with an indifferent gaze.

Shadows were massing in the laboratory. Rain pattered on the panes of the arched window. The embers of the furnace, which projected a red light, could be heard crackling amid the retorts. Occasional drops of water fell from the humid vault, and whenever one of them touched the Demon, steam and a hissing sound advertised the fact.

"Decide, Doctor," said Mephistopheles. "Once again, what do you need? It's not that I'm in a hurry; eternity awaits me—but I'm as fearful of catching a chill as anyone else. Then again, I've warned you—if you meditate for as much as another quarter-hour, the armchair will be burned through, and you'll have to get it repaired, or sit on the trunk..."

The indecisive Faust, his arm extended upon a thick table-top, mechanically rotated the cup that was filled with the poisoned beverage.

"You have a famous flaw," Mephistopheles went on. "And that, meaning no insult, is thinking too much. My word, you've cut a hair from a woman's head into four—which is quite remarkable, in this day and age."

Perplexed, Faust ran through the notions of his philosophy in his head. What should he ask for, by virtue of the pact? The fulfillment of what wish would restore his desire to live?"

"I'm off!" said the Devil, getting up. "*Au revoir*, Doctor—I'll come back another time. Between now and then, you'll have come to a decision."

"No!" cried the thinker. "Stay! Just a moment! One more moment!"

"All right!" accepted the Devil, sitting down again.

Faust offered him a chocolate box. "Would you like a bonbon?" he asked.

"Gladly." Neglecting the candy, however, the Devil delicately selected a still-ardent ember and crunched it between his teeth.

Shrugging his shoulders, Faust murmured: "Show-off!"

And nothing more was heard, save for the downpour and the furnace.

To distract himself, Mephitopheles drew smoking arabesques on the arm of the chair with the tip of his claw. "Pyrogravure," he said, improvising the word.

"Pardon?" said Faust.

"Nothing, Doctor. Anticipation."

"No more whimsy—I've found it!"

"Archimedes said that in Greek."

"I know what I want!"

"Go on."

"Youth."

"Damnation, Monsieur! Anything but that!"

"More than that," said Faust, with a penetrating gaze.

"More than that?" sad the Evil One, bewildered. "Me!"

"What do you mean by that 'Me!' Master of Obscurity?"

"I said 'Me!' as you might say 'The Devil!' And you must recognize that one might swear for less. What! Youth and more than youth!"

"Listen," Faust retorted. "If I were an old man, an old man abandoned by desire, you know as well as I do that the recovery of youth would have no attraction in my eyes. But I'm fifty-eight years old, if I'm not mistaken, and my soul is often troubled by desires that the state of my body prevents me from satisfying . . ."

"Yes," the Devil interrupted, with a smile that might have been described as licentious, "but youth alone . . ."

Faust stamped his foot. "Incorrigible goat!" he protested. "Understand me, then! The best part of youth is neither its strength nor its seduction, but the future that extends before it!"

"In truth," Mephistopheles remarked, "it's you that's being obscure. I know a witch who can give you back your twenties. Do you consent? With that done, what will your happiness lack?"

"The consciousness of being young. The sentiment of the future. I remember, you know. I was handsome. My limbs were powerful, my brain contained a world. Life and happiness were the same thing. But listen: *I didn't appreciate it*. Young men don't know . . . the joy of their spring-time is unknown to them, O my guest, until the first snows of their winter fall. And it's only today that all the grace of my past is resplendent in my old memory. For one does not know that one is young; and does that which one does not know really exist?"

"In brief," Mephistopheles concluded, "you want to be young and not to be young at the same time. You're a wise man and a madman. Wise, when you imagine the dream of which you speak, mad when you want to realize it. Oh, Monsieur! To enclose your soul, full of experience, in the dazzling flesh of a juvenile body! To make, in combination, knowledgeable youth and powerful old age! What an admirable monster you would be within Creation! But don't you think that such a prodigy is impossible, even for . . . the Other, up there, who did not wish that the color black could become white and yet remain black?" And as Faust remained somber, he added: "Come on, Doctor, it's not that I'm reluctant to perform. A pact is a pact—but no one can do the impossible. And if I were to give you some advice—listen to me, in your turn—then you must choose: either one is young, without, as you put it, knowing it, or one is no longer young, and able to savor one's youth. Which will you plump for, in the end? To recover your twenties without taking pleasure therein, or to remember gladly having lived them?"

Discouraged by a sullen silence, he made a dismissive gesture, and took a few steps away.

"*Prosit!*" said Faust.

The Spirit of Evil turned his head, and saw the philosopher drink a draught from the poisoned cup.

"As you please!" groaned the Devil. "Much good may it do you!" And he retired, presumably, whence he had come. No one knows how.

THE SABBAT BOW

by S. Henry Berthoud

MATHIAS WILMART was the best fiddler in the town of Hesdin. In no village for ten leagues around would people have danced with such a good heart if anyone other than Mathias Wilmart were playing the bass-viol. Thus, he was an individual of no small importance; he sat down at the relatives' table at weddings; the bride—who, following local custom, served the guests during the meal—never failed to give him the choice morsel. Furthermore, when he began to speak, everyone lent him their ears, for no one knew better than he did how to tell a story, sing a song or make a witty remark.

One winter evening, there was a wedding in Auffin. The dancing went on very late, and night had fallen long ago when Mathias, loading his bass-viol, which he had played with so much talent, on to his back, announced that he was going to go. All imaginable efforts were made to dissuade him from that resolution.

"Stay with us, Père Mathias," everyone said, "the wind's blowing cold; there's a frost to crack stones; the forest of Hesdrin, which you have to pass through, doesn't enjoy a good reputation; it's a haunt of wolves and highwaymen, who are no less dangerous, not to mention witches, who come to hold their Sabbats there."

"I have a goblet of excellent wine in my belly," the stubborn old man replied, "a good fur cloak covers my shoulders, and here's a stout iron-tipped staff in my hand. With that I can defy the cold, the wolves and the thieves. As for witches and devils, if I meet any, I'll make them dance to the music of my bass-viol. Why, they can tell me whether the fiddlers in Hell can ply the bow as well as Mathias Wilmart of Hedrin!"

He had scarcely been on the road for a quarter of an hour when the sky, starry until then, was suddenly covered by immense clouds. The darkness became terrifying. Then the fiddler surprised himself by regretting the good bed that he had been offered in Auffin—but it was too late to retrace his steps. Besides which, after the boasts he had made, they would be bound to mock him, saying that fear had brought him back. So he continued walking. To cap his chagrin, it did not take him long to notice that he had gone astray.

What should he do? To keep going might only be to go further astray. To wrap himself up in his cloak and lie down at the foot of a tree did not appear to be a safe thing to do; the wolves would undoubtedly come to rip out his throat; besides which, if he escaped the carnivorous beasts, he would surely perish of the cold. Meanwhile, with both hands gripping his staff, he remained in a state of painful anxiety; then a light suddenly appeared in the distance.

It's shining in some woodcutter's hut, he said to himself. *Thank God!*

He tried to head in the direction in which the light was shining, but it had disappeared. He struck the ground with his iron-tipped staff and uttered a horrible blasphemy. The guilty words were scarcely out of his mouth when the light reappeared.

It was not without much difficulty and after a long and perilous journey that Mathias reached the place from which the light toward which he had been marching for so long was coming. His surprise became extreme when he arrived, for he found himself outside a château of magnificent appearance, of which he had never heard mention. Lively music was resounding there in all its parts, and the dancers who were continually passing in front of the windows cast their swift black shadows on the curtains, which were rendered translucent by a red glare.

He circled around the immense building several times, but in vain, searching for the entrance door. He was despairing of finding it when an old man suddenly appeared and started blowing a horn. A drawbridge, which Mathias had not seen until then, was abruptly lowered, and the fiddler, following the old man, went into the manor.

He was utterly astonished to find it filled with an inconceivable multitude of people. Some were taking part in a splendid feast, others were playing games of chance, but the largest number were dancing and uttering deafening cries.

Mathias marched boldly toward a tall man whom he recognized as the master of the abode by the manner in which he was giving orders and the respect with which he was treated.

"Lord Castellan," he said, "I'm a poor fiddler lost in the woods; deign to permit me to spend the night in a corner of your manor; I'll leave tomorrow at daybreak."

The individual to whom Mathias was speaking only replied with a benevolent gesture of assent. On his order, a page took the fiddler's bass-viol and hung it on one of the golden nails shining in the rich wall-hanging of the room. While he attended to this task the page smiled in a strange manner, and the place where his hand touched the instrument immediately blackened, as if the hand were made of fire.

Mathias began parading his gaze around and examining the place in which he found himself, but he sought in vain to recognize any of the people surrounding him; every time he fixed his eyes on the face of one of them, a kind of light mist veiled the face in question and deceived the old man's curiosity. While he was trying to fathom this prodigy, he perceived a bass-viol, and the instrument seemed to him to be so beautiful that the desire gripped him to make use of it and go to play with the other fiddlers, to whom he would not be sorry to demonstrate his skill. As he raised his eyes to look for the staircase that would take him up to their gallery, however, he was astounded to recognize among them Barnabé Malassart, who had died thirty years before, and who had given him his first lessons on the bass-viol,

"Holy Virgin have pity on me!" he exclaimed.

At the same instant, everything—the musicians, the dancers and the château—vanished before his eyes.

The next day, the people of Auffin who, more prudent than the fiddler, had deferred the day of their departure for the town, found the poor man lying unconscious at the foot of the gibbet, with a white bow in his hand.

"Père Mathias," one of them said, "has chosen to sleep in a rather unattractive location."

"And an even less attractive nail on which to hang his bass-viol," another replied. "Look—the bass-viol and the bow are attached to the big toe of the foot of a hanged man."

"Was he afraid that the cadaver might be cold?" asked a third. "He's covered its desiccated shoulders with his cloak."

"He's a careful man, Père Mathias," added a fourth, who was attempting to revive the old musician. "He'd brought two bows, in order not to be left short id one of them happened to break."

Having come round, thanks to the care lavished on him, Mathias put the blame for his accident on the cold and was careful not to say a word about the infernal visions that he had experienced during the night.

When he got home, however, he carefully examined the bow of which he had become the possessor in such a strange manner. A frisson of terror followed that examination. The bow was nothing but the bone of a dead man, carved with extreme care; one could also read in its rich silver ornamentation the name of a resident of Hesdin who was reputed in the town, with good reason, to be a spell-caster and sorcerer.

Mathias waited for nightfall and then went to the house of the man of ill-repute.

"Neighbor," be said, bowing deeply, "this is a bow that belongs to you, I think. I found it by chance and I'm returning it to you."

The neighbor went pale at these words, and stood there momentarily without saying a word, so great was his emotion.

"Uh oh, Mathias!" he finally murmured. "You've discovered that singular things happen by night, and a word from you could do me harm."

"May God please that I don't speak it, Neighbor!"

"You're a worthy man, Mathias, but you'd do well to keep silent. If I'm burned alive—which they would surely do if they knew that you'd seen me you-know-where—something bad might happen to you."

Mathias got up to go, but the owner of the bow made him sit down again, and moved nearer in order to whisper in his ear in a very low voice: "Neighbor, tell me who your enemies are; I'll cast a spell on their livestock tonight, or I'll give them some wasting disease that will rid you of them."

"I have no enemies, Neighbor, and may God please that I wish no evil on my peers!"

"In what way can I be useful to you, then?"

"In none, Neighbor," the fiddler replied, already wishing that he was outside. "None at all. I'm just glad to have been able to return such a beautiful bow to you."

"A very precious bow, to be sure—but it's necessary that I make you a gift, Père Mathias."

"Give him this purse—no matter how hard he tries to empty it, it will always contain six Parisian francs in solid money."

These words had been pronounced by a man with a sinister face, who had certainly not been in the sorcerer's study when Mathias arrived there. How had he got in? That was incomprehensible, for the doors had been carefully closed by the master of the house, in order that his conversation with Mathias could not be overheard.

"This is some work of the evil spirit," exclaimed the fiddler, "and I won't risk my salvation by accepting it!"

"It's a talisman," replied the unknown individual. "A talisman of which a Christian can make use without fear." As he pronounced the word "Christian" a frisson ran through all his limbs. He added, laughing bitterly: "If this purse is the Devil's work, then I'm damned!"

Half-reassured, Mathias succumbed to the temptation of becoming the possessor of such a treasure.

He emptied the marvelous purse so often that he soon acquired a nice house, and started to live as the richest townsfolk of Hesdin were able to do. Every day there were parties and feasts that never ended. He continued to play for the dancers at weddings, but he now had a good mule to take him to the homes of the newlyweds, which walked at a brisk pace, and a servant to carry his bass-viol.

The fiddler's new lifestyle excited considerable comment in the town of Hesdin. The most general rumor alleged that Mathias had found an immense treasure, which he kept hidden in some secret place in his house.

Now, Mathias had four nephews, bad lots of whose conduct no good had ever come. One day, they said to one another: "Uncle Mathias has become rich; there's no one but us to inherit his great wealth . . ."

Apparently, one word suffices for scoundrels to understand one another, for they each went home to fetch an arbalest, and came back to hide at a crossroads in the woods through which Mathias was due to pass that evening.

The fiddler was unable to avoid his destiny; four arbalest darts struck him dead; his servant, who was luckier, ran away.

Without giving any thought to the witness to their crime, the four brothers ran to the cadaver to rob it, expecting to share the inheritance. A tall man with a sinister face stopped them, leapt upon the corpse, took a small purse from the dead man's wallet and disappeared, shouting: "That's how people profit from my gifts!"

Execrable laughter followed those words.

While the murderers stood there, motionless and bewildered, the provost of law and his archers suddenly surrounded them.

Mathias' servant had met them in the woods as he fled and had come to deliver his master's murderers to them.

Given the evidence of the crime, justice was not slow in being rendered to them. The provost had the rascals hanged from the trees behind which they had hidden, arbalests in hand—for which reason the place in question is known today as the Crossroads of the Four Brothers.

FAUST'S GRANDSON

by Félicien Champsaur

HE had just attended a performance of Gounod's masterpiece, *Faust*. After a trip to the club, where he had ended up losing the last of his money, the grandson of the celebrated doctor went home very sad, for he was in love with Alice Penthièvre, and, after the performance, he had seen her climb into a cab with her old ape. Yes, she had left him for a player on the Bourse who, having profited to the tune of a million and a half in his speculations on the famous Societé Bontoux, had had a good enough nose to sniff the impending collapse and liquidate.

On emerging from the gambling den, Faust's grandson had admired the moon, like a *louis d'or* cast into the night, a discreet procuress drawing the starry curtain over the amorous, and now he was writing a sonnet whose rhymes had buzzed in his cranium as he walked through the streets:

The Battles of Life[1]

Twenty, at the most, sleeping beside an old man
Greedy for her soft skin and brazen attitude;
Her long blonde hair, and her body, in the nude
Extends languidly for him on the soft divan.

The darling's bag is stuffed by a financier
Almost impotent, who found her flat broke;
But the métier's hard, enough to choke
The blonde, fed up with something chancier.

She has to earn that house on the avenue
The little whore, adorable and true,
Trying in vain her old lover to excite.

Will she be disgusted by the old gray beard
And the groping of virility disappeared
When she wakes in the morning after tonight?

When he had finished the last line, with his elbows on the table and his head in his hands, he thought at first of the folly of millions agitating Paris, and then about his ancestor.

People are no longer as naive as that doctor. He claimed to know everything: philosophy, law, medicine and theology too, but if he had another distraction in his work than

---

1 Because the story specifically refers to the sonnet's rhymes I have contrived a version that retains the rhyme-scheme rather than translating each line literally, hopefully reproducing the spirit and doggerel quality of the original.

invoking Phoebe, summoning her mild and melancholy
amity, if he had studied life, instead of poring, almost inces-
santly, over dusty books, he would not have demanded that
Mephistopheles, in exchange for his soul, give him youth.
When the Devil offered him a fortune, the doctor had not
insults enough for gold and its pleasures.

Youth has all the privileges? Those who imagine that
can look to see whether they have gold coins in their pockets
and banknotes in their wallet . . . Supernatural apparitions
are no longer abreast of the times, for if the Devil consented
to show himself now, Faust's grandson would gladly sell
him any soul he might have in order to obtain opulence
and old age.

As he was reflecting in that fashion, he heard a light
sound of footsteps and, directing his gaze toward the entrance door, he perceived a very distinguished stranger,
who, after bowing, approached him and handed him a
card, on which were engraved, beneath a closed crown,
the words:

Prince de Satan

The young man invited the visitor to sit down and
presented him with a box of cigars, inviting him to take
one.

"Forgive me, Monsieur," he added, "but what proof
do I have that you really are the Devil?"

Satan took a few state-manufactured matches from
the mantelpiece and, strike after strike, lit seven of them
in succession.

It was extraordinary.

Faust's grandson, convinced by that evident manifestation of a superior and mysterious power, spoke in the following terms:

"My grandfather, who had the honor of making a deal with you, delivered his soul to you in exchange for your having rendered him young, in answer to his desire. He was able to be content to flirt with Marguerite and see—which he would not have been able to do when he was buried in his books—more charms in her half-closed eyelids and her fresh lips than in all the wisdom in the world. I, Faust's grandson, am young, and yet I don't esteem that it's much preferable to having lived.

"A man, during his childhood, is ignorant of everything. Afterwards, he uses up his youth, and also his maturity, in efforts that are sometimes not crowned with success, in order to acquire comfort and fortune for his old age. An employee obtains his retirement—which is to say, happiness—after thirty years of submission and regularity. A merchant becomes a rentier after wasting the best part of his existence in a shop. A soldier receives, when it is too late, the epaulettes of a general admired by beautiful ladies and saluted by gentlemen. An artist, painter, musician, writer or sculptor, does not have renown or success, and, above all, does not possess the fortune for which he dreamed in order to satisfy his aristocratic caprices—for any artist worthy of the name is an aristocrat—until his hair turns white, when his youth has fled, many winters ago, weeping in the midst of illusions.

"That is why, Monsieur, little desirous of remaining in difficulty, impatient to arrive at enjoyment and the goal, I would be delighted, if you could grant it to me—

of which I have no doubt—to be respectably old and a millionaire, immediately."

Mephistopheles, who was smoking his cigar, had listened to Faust's grandson in the most polite fashion, for he had lent him scrupulous attention; but he had certainly known in advance everything that the young man had to confide in him. In a familiar tone, he said:

"I divine, my dear fellow, that you are under the hammer of the eternal question of amour and money. You have spent quite a bit of money, thirty thousand francs—all that you had—in a month, on Alice Penthièvre of the Avenue de Messine, and, as you are now cleaned out, you have been surpassed.

"You are not one of those lovers who go in via the kitchen and up by the service stairway. I congratulate you all the more for that, as I am glad to inform you that it has been decided this evening in the Council of Ministers—which I attended in the skin of Monsieur Grévy[1]—that the Prefect of Police will be given the mission of purging Paris of at least ten thousand pimps. The project has been drawn up of forming three exceptional regiments, which will be sent overseas in order to terminate the Tonkin affair. They will, moreover, retain their distinctive character and will have a superb tightly-fitting green costume, brandeburgs and tall helmets. Grévin[2] will design the uniforms for the three regiments. That way, we shall put an end to those ridiculous Chinamen. If Monsieur Grévy accepts the Council's decision, the

---

1 Jules Grévy was the President of the Republic from 1879-1887.
2 The caricaturist Alfred Grévin (1827-1892) was also a prolific designer of theatrical costumes.

foreign news section of the newspapers will soon be full of reports of triumphs: *Great naval combat. The three-tier helmets continue to cover themselves with glory* . . .

"In Paris, as you see, my dear, the Devil must be everywhere. It's exhausting, take my word for it. But let's get back to our affair. You want to be immensely rich. Doubtless in order that the slightest caprices of one or several women can be executed; you want to be opulent and old right away. I consent to that. What will you cede to me in return?"

"My soul. It will be deliverable to you by contract, whenever it pleases God to separate it from my body."

Satan forgot all discretion and uttered a burst of laughter in a shrill note.

"Your soul, did you say? That's too droll. Let's try to talk a little more seriously, shall we?"

He went on:

"The soul exists. It is tradeable, but the stock is not high. Once, a hundred years ago, I speculated a great deal on that commodity. Souls went from five hundred francs to seven hundred, then twelve hundred, and finally to three thousand. However, I went through severe crises without flinching when Locke, Condillac and Kant, who searched for the soul in the fluid contained in the cerebral cavities, declared that every idea is a continued sensation, and when Voltaire said, smiling, that *soul* is a word invented to express, confusedly and obscurely, the mechanisms of our life.

"I resisted all those attacks, but then came, after those of Cabanis, the experiments of Magendie and Flourens, those of Sir John Lubbock, Bain and Huxley in England, of Berthelot, Broca, Robin, Vulpian and d'Orbigny in France. Friedreich wrote that the same force that digests via the stomach thinks via the brain, Littré that mind is a property of the nervous substance, as gravitation is of every material particle ...

"A collapse was threatened. I should have suspected as much; souls crashed. I took a heavy hit. But I have the stomach and I absorbed the blow. Even so, a scalded Devil fears cold water. I don't want your soul! Why do these so-called scientists have so much influence? From first to last, though, they're only spinning out, in bad prose, this distich from the grotesque poet Cyrano de Bergerac:

An hour after death, our soul is in dearth,
Become what it was an hour before birth.

"You'll understand, therefore, that I can't accept your soul, since it's distinction from the body is, for humans, a simple analytical procedure. But I can take your youth. You have twenty years, black and supple hair, soft and energetic eyes. If you wish, I'll acquire all of that, in order to lead astray some chaste girl—not on earth, of course, for no young woman here any longer believes in silliness, and virgins here no longer allow themselves to be cajoled by sweet talk, but on other worlds that are more backward than your planet and chimeras have not yet become ridiculous ...

"In return for the abandonment you make me, you'll obtain what you would scarcely have had, by dint of labor, in thirty years: old age and fortune. The means is facile. I've always known what scientists would eventually discover after centuries. Claude Bernard explains, in his studies on the problem of physiology, that by injecting oxygenated blood via the carotid into the head of a decapitated dog, one sees the vital properties of the muscles, glands, nerves and the brain slowly return. If you permit me to operate, my dear, *in anima nobile*, I can oxygenate you to the point of saturation and you'll live forty years in the space of five minutes . . .

"Will you sell me your youth? I hope to utilize that cast-off clothing on one of the other planets rotating around your sun."

After a silence, the young man said:

"I'll gladly accept to be old and to possess for myself alone the beloved who is escaping me . . . Penthièvre—which astonishes me, for she has intelligence—is capable, then, of sticking to me . . . By the way, you know, I don't want an inconvenient passion. It's sufficient that I find a tranquil and delightful amour in the evening, at ten or eleven o'clock, after the club."

"As you please."

"Shall we sign the pact, then?"

So Faust's grandson sold his youth, was sixty years old and, what is more, stole Alice Penthièvre from the stock-market trader enriched by Monsieur Bontoux's disaster. His blonde lover deceived him with a young assistant stockbroker, but as he never knew anything about it, he was very happy.

And he even remained young, because, as soon as she saw them appear, she plucked out his white hairs.

ACKNOWLEDGEMENTS

S. HENRY BERTHOUD was the signature employed for most of his writings by Samuel-Henri Berthoud (1804-1919), whose long career stretched from pioneering involvement in the Romantic Movement as an editor and writer to the prolific production of educational material for children and the popularization of science. "La Partie d'échecs du diable" and "L'Archet du sabbat" both appeared in *Chroniques et traditions surnaturelles de la Flandre* (1831) and were reprinted, along with "La Sonate du diable" in *Légendes et traditions surnaturelles des Flandres [sic]* (1862). All three translations first appeared in *Martyrs of Science and Other Victims of Devilry and Destiny* (2013).

FÉLICIEN CHAMPSAUR (1858-1934) began his career as a key contributor to the Decadent Movement, and retained an outré Decadent element in his works when he became a best-selling novelist with such works as *L'Amant des danseuse* (1888) and *L'Orgie latine* (1903; tr. as *The Latin Orgy*). "Le Petit-fils de Faust" appeared in the collection *Entrée de Clowns* (1886); "Faust's Grandson" first appeared in *The Emerald Princess and Other Decadent Fantasies* (2017).

LUCIE DELARUE-MARDRUS (1874-1945) was a prolific poet, sculptor, novelist and journalist who was a regular contributor to *Le Journal* for forty years. She was married to the physician and Oriental scholar J. C. Mardrus between 1900 and 1915 but was also an intimate member of Natalie Barney's circle, along with Renée Vivien, and was awarded the first Renée Vivien prize for poetry in 1936. "La Femme aux enfers" was first published in *Le Journal*, 13 June 1913; "A Woman in Hell" first appeared in *The Last Siren and Other Stories* (2021).

GUSTAVE FLAUBERT (1821-1880) was a notorious perfectionist, and hence not very prolific, but he made cardinal contributions to three genres of fiction in the ground-breaking naturalistic novel *Madame Bovary* (1857), the lush historical fantasy *Salammbô* (1862) and the phantasmagorical philosophical fantasy *La Tentation de Saint-Antoine* (1874). The posthumously-published "Rêve d'enfer" was written in 1837, when the author was sixteen years old. "A Dream of Hell" is original to the present collection.

LÉON GOZLAN (1803-1866) was a prolific novelist whose career began in his teens with the oft-reprinted satire *Les Émotions de Polydore Marasquin* (1820; tr. as *The Emotions of Polydore Marasquin*), about a man cast away on an island inhabited by intelligent apes, who briefly becomes their ruler. "Encore une âme vendue au diable" was first published in two parts in the *Bulletin de l'ami des arts* in 1844. "Another Soul Sold to the Devil" first appeared in *The Vampire of the Val-de-Grace* (2012).

JULES JANIN (1804-1874) worked alongside S. Henry Berthoud as an editor of and contributor to periodicals launched by Émile Girardin, which lent considerable impetus to the Romantic Movement in the late 1820s and 1830s. His *L'Âne mort et la femme guillotinée* (1829; tr. as *The Dead Donkey and the Guillotined Woman*) was one of the classic novels of the Movement. "Tout de bon Coeur," written in 1826, was collected posthumously in *Contes, nouvelles et récits* (1885); the translation, "Sincerity" first appeared in *The Magnetized Corpse and Other Paradoxical Tales* (2014).

CATULLE MENDÈS (1841-1909) was taken under the wing of Théophile Gautier when he first came to Paris. His unproduced drama *Roman d'une nuit* (1861) was prosecuted for obscenity, landing him in prison for a month. He was extraordinarily adaptable and prolific, producing an enormous amount of short fiction for newspapers. His novels *Zo'har* (1886) and *Méphistophela* (1890; tr. as *Mephistophela*) were crucial contributions to the Decadent Movement. "Larmes brûlée" appeared in *Arc-en-ciel et sourcil-rouge* (1897); "Burned Tears" appeared in *Don Juan in Paradise and Other Amorous Fantasies* (2019).

CHARLES NODIER (1780-1844) was one of the pioneers of French Romantic prose; his salon at the Bibliothèque de l'Arsenal, begun in 1824 and known as *Le Cénacle*, brought together many of the key figures in the Movement and spun off other *cénacles* in which it was anchored, including Victor Hugo's. His best work consists of short stories and novellas. "La Combe de l'homme mort" first appeared in the eleventh volume of *Le Salmigondis, contes de tous les couleurs* in 1833; the translation is original to the present collection.

PIERRE-ALEXIS PONSON DU TERRAIL (1829-1871) became one of the stars of the *roman feuilleton* under the Second Empire, in competition with Paul Féval, sometimes writing five serials simultaneously, most famously chronicling the career of the flamboyant adventurer Rocambole. "Une Légende fatale" was frst published in the *Bulletin de la Societé des gens de lettres* in 1854. "A Fatal Legend" first appeared in *The Chambrion and Other Stories* (2013).

JEAN RICHEPIN (1849-1926) was one of the more flamboyant figures of *fin-de-siècle* Paris, a star of the impromptu cabaret of Le Chat Noir. Best known for his songs and dramas, he was affectionately accused by Sarah Bernhardt of being a bigger ham than she was. He was freakishly elected to the Académie Française, apparently as a result of a cabal determined to sabotage Henri de Régnier's election. "L'Horloge" first appeared in *Le Journal* 14 March 1900; "The Clock" first appeared in *The Crazy Corner: Horrible Stories* (2013).

PIERRE VÉRON (1833-1900) was one of the most successful French humorists of the nineteenth century, a leading contributor to *Le Charivari* and *Le Journal amusant*. "La Double vue" was reprinted in *Paris à tous les diables* (1874). "Second Sight" first appeared in *The Merchants of Health and Other Fantastic Stories* (2015).

A PARTIAL LIST OF SNUGGLY BOOKS